# THE TROUBLE WITH TWINS

Arabella

Henrietta

# THE Trouble WITH Twins

## KATHRYN SIEBEL

With illustrations by
### JÚLIA SARDÀ

A YEARLING BOOK

Text copyright © 2016 by Kathryn Siebel
Cover art and interior illustrations copyright © 2016 by Júlia Sardà

All rights reserved. Published in the United States by Yearling, an imprint of Random House Children's Books, a division of Penguin Random House LLC, New York. Originally published in hardcover in the United States by Alfred A. Knopf, an imprint of Random House Children's Books, New York, in 2016.

Yearling and the jumping horse design are registered trademarks of Penguin Random House LLC.

Visit us on the Web! rhcbooks.com

Educators and librarians, for a variety of teaching tools, visit us at RHTeachersLibrarians.com

The Library of Congress has cataloged the hardcover edition of this work as follows:
Siebel, Kathryn.
The trouble with twins / Kathryn Siebel ; with illustrations by Júlia Sardà. — First edition.
p. cm.
Summary: When twin sisters become separated after a big fight, their strong sense of attachment leads them to find one another again.
ISBN 978-1-101-93273-5 (trade) — ISBN 978-1-101-93274-2 (lib. bdg.) — ISBN 978-1-101-93275-9 (ebook)
[1. Sisters—Fiction. 2. Twins—Fiction. 3. Separation (Psychology)—Fiction.] I. Title.
PZ7.1.S53 Tr 2016
[Fic]—dc23
2015013541

ISBN 978-1-101-93276-6 (pbk.)

Printed in the United States of America
10 9 8 7 6 5 4 3 2 1
First Yearling Edition 2018

Random House Children's Books supports the First Amendment and celebrates the right to read.

For my sisters,
Eileen and Mary,
with love

*To Any Reader*

*So you may see, if you will look*
*Through the windows of this book,*
*Another child, far, far away,*
*And in another garden, play.*

. . .

*He does not hear; he will not look,*
*Nor yet be lured out of this book.*
*For, long ago, the truth to say,*
*He has grown up and gone away,*
*And it is but a child of air*
*That lingers in the garden there.*

ROBERT LOUIS STEVENSON

# THE TROUBLE WITH TWINS

## ❧ THROUGH THE WINDOWS ❧

And so it begins in front of the fire, the story of two twin sisters. One remains with her family in their lovely country house, where yellow roses perfume the air. The other waits for her in another house, where she stands alone at huge arched windows. She is restless, pacing wooden floors that creak in the night when a cat jumps down from the bed to chase at shadows.

"What are their names?" the girl asks. "The sisters."

"Arabella and Henrietta."

"Are they lonely?" asks the girl.

"They belong together," says the mother. "And it makes them sad to be apart."

"Can't you tell a happy story?" the girl asks.

"With puppies and a garden?"

"Yes!" says the girl.

"I'm only telling it the way my mother told it to me," the mother says.

"And will there be puppies?" the girl persists. "Or only gloomy girls at windows?"

"Well, their dog, Muffin, wasn't exactly a puppy, but she was very small. And, there was a beautiful garden. I can picture it perfectly. But we should start at the beginning."

## ❧ TWO SISTERS ❧

Henrietta and Arabella Osgood were born on the second and third days of April. When they were little, they were everything to each other. They slept in the same crib and wore matching baby outfits. They dreamed the same dreams and played together. People said they learned to talk their own secret language that no one else could understand. They were both beautiful girls, but from the start Arabella was somehow more beautiful than Henrietta. And that is where the trouble began.

Since everyone knew they were twins, nobody could understand why they seemed so different. Arabella was always smiling and laughing, her pink cheeks creased by deep dimples, a charming gap between her two front teeth. Her clothes were spotless, and her glossy blond hair was perfectly combed. Every day their nanny, Rose, arranged it in a new and elaborate hairstyle, tying off the ends with bits of colorful ribbon that blew gently in the breeze.

Henrietta, on the other hand, was as quiet and serious as an elderly professor. She seldom spoke, rarely smiled. Crumbs tumbled down the front of her clothes. And her hair! Well, Rose always meant to get to it, but she had such fun fixing Arabella's that she never did.

Their differences had never mattered to the two of them, but they had always influenced how others treated them. When they were babies, Rose always fed Arabella first and held her more. When they grew older, Arabella was the one the girls' parents asked to perform for guests. Arabella would recite a poem or sing a song for the grown-ups before they went off to dinner. The adults would smile at her and clap their hands in delight, and they barely noticed Henrietta as they passed her on the way to the dining room. And even when nobody else was around, Mr. and Mrs. Osgood were always praising Arabella. "Have you ever seen such blue eyes?" they would ask each other, gazing fondly at Arabella. "Doesn't she have the most delicate fingers? Born to play the harp." Of course they were never mean to Henrietta. At least not at first. But it was clear to everyone who ever met them that the Osgoods liked Arabella best. Watching them fawn over Arabella, Henrietta stood back, saying nothing and feeling too much.

At school the girls sat near each other: Arabella at a clean, perfect desk from which she unfailingly gave the right answer, and Henrietta at an older one with gum under the seat. Inside were forgotten peanut butter and jelly sandwiches that Henrietta hadn't wanted to eat and smudgy homework papers that showed, as her teacher Mr. Stilton-Sterne was always saying, that Henrietta couldn't be paying very much attention.

Outside the house, Arabella was always busy with friends. The other girls invited Arabella to their birthday parties, where they ate tiny, delicious chocolate candies from pink paper cups under birthday streamers and balloons. On the playground, they hopscotched together and gathered in tight circles, giggling, whispering, and pulling up their socks. Arabella didn't mean to leave Henrietta out of all the fun; she just seemed to lose track of her sister, and Henrietta had to either find someone else to skip rope with or make peace with standing off in a corner all alone.

But at home they built their own world. They lined up dolls and stuffed bears, poured them invisible tea, and invented their conversation. When the sun shone, they dressed each other in their mother's old dresses; they added paper crowns and wings and ran through the garden, playing fairy princess. When it rained, their heads were bent over drawing paper as they passed crayons to and fro in companionable silence. They were mirror images, touchstones. The sight of the other steadied each of them. They ate the same meals, listened to the same conversations between their parents at dinner, received the same gifts in different colors. Both

sisters knew with a look what the other was thinking, and words were seldom necessary. They ended each day whispering good night across the short space between their matching beds.

Yet as soon as they arrived at school every morning, things changed. There was so much more going on there, and Arabella was always at the center of it all, encircled by her adoring friends. Henrietta, on the other hand, spent her days by the wrought-iron fence on the edges of the playground, staring at Arabella and her friends.

"Mother," asks the girl by the fire, "if Arabella and Henrietta are twins, how could they be born on different days?"

"It does happen sometimes," the mother insists. "Henrietta was born just before midnight at the end of April second. And Arabella was born a bit after, in the wee hours of April third."

"Well, that's very unusual, don't you think?"

"They were very unusual sisters."

"And that bit about dreaming the same dreams. How could anyone know that?" the girl asks.

"I know these two girls quite well," the mother says. "Do you want to hear their story or not?"

## THE LAST STRAW

For her part, Arabella was blissfully ignorant of how deeply unhappy her sister was. She knew, of course, that Henrietta was quiet and odd—that she stood apart from things. But it would have surprised and saddened her to know the extent of her sister's suffering. And Henrietta couldn't bring herself to confront Arabella directly—at least not at first. Her resentment was a secret tangle coiled deep inside her, and it went unseen for years until one day an argument and some unkind words finally nudged Henrietta toward action.

The girls had been playing hide-and-seek together. The

game had gone on longer than usual—in part because of a light rain that discouraged going outdoors, but also because of some especially creative hiding places and a bit of assistance from Rose. Henrietta crept across the kitchen on tiptoe.

"Where is she?" Henrietta whispered to the nanny.

"I'll never tell," Rose declared as she arranged some fruit on a plate.

Then Rose glanced at the kitchen clock and said, "Oh dear, it's nearly two. Arabella! You best come out, or you'll be late!"

"I win!" Arabella declared cheerfully as she stepped out of the pantry closet.

"You don't win," Henrietta protested. "And you have flour all over your face."

"We'd better get you cleaned up," said Rose. "You'll be late for the party."

Arabella, it seemed, had been invited to yet another birthday party—this one for a girl named Lacey.

"Here," said Rose, handing the plate of sliced apples to Henrietta like a consolation prize. "Have a snack."

"But we're in the middle of a game," said Henrietta. "You can't just leave."

Arabella sighed. "I told you before. Lacey's birthday party is this afternoon."

Perhaps she *had* said something. Arabella's schedule was full of wonderful things: parties and piano lessons and ballet classes. All Henrietta ever did was bite her fingernails, meet with her tutor, and wait for Arabella to come home.

"Remember?" Arabella asked. "I showed you the present I got for her. The doll?"

Now Henrietta remembered the shiny package topped by a blue bow that waited in the front hall.

"Well, when will you be back?" Henrietta asked. "I thought when we were done with hide-and-seek, we could work on the puzzle."

"I know!" Arabella said. "But, Henrietta, be reasonable! I have better things to do right now than work on a jigsaw puzzle!"

"But it's a thousand pieces," Henrietta said, following her sister to their room and watching as Rose slipped a party dress over Arabella's head. "How am I supposed to do it alone?" Henrietta asked.

The two girls often worked on puzzles in the evening while their mother painted and their father read the newspaper. They had been piecing this one together for days—connecting bits of blue sky and the bright yellow flowers that reminded them of their mother's garden. Now it lay half-finished on a low table in the living room, and Arabella had lost all interest.

"Come on, Bella Bella," Henrietta coaxed. "Please?"

Finally the pressure was too much for Arabella, but instead of giving in (as she often did), Arabella snapped at her twin.

"Henrietta, you're making me late!" Arabella yelled as she buckled her patent leather shoes. "I'll miss the best parts. But I guess you wouldn't understand that, since you never leave the house."

"I go places!" Henrietta shouted back, though she couldn't think of any. "I have friends!" Henrietta insisted, though none came to mind.

"Oh, Henrietta," Arabella sighed. "You'll think of something to keep yourself busy. You always do. I have to go. I have to get this doll to Lacey. It's her birthday."

"Fine!" Henrietta yelled. "Go! Who needs you?"

At this, Arabella's usually smiling face clouded over.

"You're mean," Arabella proclaimed. "That's why you don't have any friends."

And she marched away.

## ❧ THE PLOT THICKENS ☙

For a few days after Lacey's birthday party, the girls barely spoke.

"Do you want a piece of toast?" Arabella would ask crisply as she passed her sister the plate at breakfast.

The only reply from Henrietta was a dark stare.

"Henrietta!" her mother scolded. "Your sister is asking you a question."

"No," Henrietta said.

"No thank you," her mother prompted.

"Never mind, Mother," Arabella said.

And so it went.

At times they would forget their feud, unaccustomed to fighting as they were. Arabella saved a cupcake that was passed out in class one day, meaning to split it with her sister later. Then she remembered that they were now mortal enemies and licked off the pink icing all by herself, feeling teary. And it was the same for Henrietta, who would store up some story or joke from the school day, meaning to share it later with her sister—until she remembered that they were no longer speaking. These lost opportunities only made them more furious in some strange way, and each was determined not to be the first to give in and apologize. Their quarrel was their newest project, like a puzzle they were solving, and each one added to it—piece by piece.

Arabella no longer helped Henrietta find missing homework or shoes as they got ready for school in the morning. Instead, she yelled to her mother, "Henrietta is making us late again!" And for her part, Henrietta spent a great deal of time dreaming up ways to punish her sister for her disloyalty. Until one day, as she sat in the parlor reading a book, Henrietta overheard her parents saying something that gave her an idea.

"Where have you been off to?" Mrs. Osgood asked her husband.

"Went to the barber," he said as he took off his hat.

"Little short, don't you think?"

"Perhaps it is a bit," he said, turning his head as he studied his reflection in the hall mirror next to the hat stand.

"What do you think, Henrietta?"

Henrietta set the book down and was about to answer when her mother interrupted, "Oh, what does she know! She's just a child. I'd try another barber if I were you."

From across the room, Henrietta considered her father's hair. It did look a little choppy. "I've got it!" she thought triumphantly. And she went off to her mother's sewing room to look for a pair of scissors. Upstairs, their bedroom was empty. Arabella was at a piano lesson. Henrietta pictured her sister's perfect blond head asleep on the pillow and was filled with secret, evil joy. So she stashed the scissors under her mattress.

"Oh my God!" the girl screams, her mouth full of cookie. "She's going to kill her!"

"Of course not," the mother says, dusting cookie crumbs off her lap. "That would be completely inappropriate. What sort of story do you think this is?"

"I don't think I want to hear the rest."

"All right," the mother says. "Whatever you prefer. It's time you were getting some rest yourself."

"Not now, thinking of people stabbed with sewing scissors."

"That isn't how the story goes."

## ☙ THE DEED IS DONE ❧

Nothing happened at first because Henrietta was such a heavy sleeper. She meant to wake up in the middle of the night and carry out her plan, but every time she would slip into some strange dream of shopping for candy or being chased by dogs, and when she woke, the sun would be coming through the window, and Rose would be shaking her shoulder and saying how if she wasn't careful she was going to be late for school again.

Mrs. Osgood noticed, one afternoon when she sat down to needlepoint, that her sewing scissors were missing. She went around the house muttering and sighing. Then she gave up and decided to work instead on a watercolor picture she was painting of her lapdog, Muffin.

"What a pretty picture!" Henrietta told her, for truly it couldn't hurt to keep her mother in a good mood. "A bunny in your garden."

"A bunny?! That's not a bunny; it's a dog. Muffin, in fact."

"Oh," said Henrietta, staring harder at the muddy swirls in the center of her mother's canvas.

Mr. Osgood, who had just walked by, stopped and gave Henrietta a worried glance.

"Does that look like a bunny to you?" Mrs. Osgood asked, turning to her husband.

"Oh, dearest, you know I can't see a thing without my new spectacles."

"Spectacles?" asks the girl.

"Glasses," says the mother.

"Where are they?" Mrs. Osgood demanded to know.

"Well, dear, that's an excellent question. I'd best find them, hadn't I? Henrietta, would you like to help?"

So Henrietta and her father backed slowly and carefully out of the room, while Mrs. Osgood went on muttering to herself. "Bunny! Preposterous. I think we need to have *your* eyes checked too, young lady!"

Knowing how easily her mother became upset, Henrietta kept a low profile as she waited for the perfect moment to use the stolen scissors. As she was falling asleep each night, she would sneak her hand down beneath the mattress to make sure that the scissors were still there, and she would smile.

At last one night she did wake up before dawn, perhaps because the light of the moon was so strong in the window. She tiptoed across to Arabella's bed. Arabella was sleeping soundly, her hair spread out across the pillow like a waterfall. Henrietta picked up a handful; her fingers shook. The scissors were small and silver in the moonlight. Henrietta dropped the handful of hair and bent over her dreaming sister. She could feel Arabella's moth breath against her cheek as she leaned in. Delicately, she lifted Arabella's bangs away from her forehead and long eyelashes. In the silence, Henrietta could hear the crisp snip of the scissors as she cut her sister's bangs. Bits of golden hair fell onto the pillowcase and slipped beneath the soft blanket. Arabella murmured and rolled over in her sleep, and Henrietta had to tiptoe to the other side of the bed to finish the job.

Henrietta was pleased with her work. Arabella's bangs were short, choppy, uneven—much worse than her father's haircut.

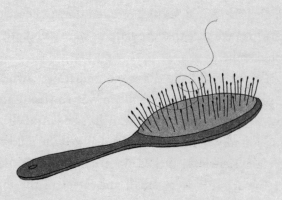

## ❧ IN THE LIGHT OF DAY ❧

The next morning, when Rose saw Arabella's crooked bangs, she became hysterical. She dropped the brush *and* the red hair ribbon she was holding.

"What have you done to your hair?" Rose wailed.

The noise sent Mrs. Osgood rushing into the room, still in her blue satin robe, demanding to know what the matter was.

"She's cut her own bangs!" Rose screamed. (You would have thought someone had been murdered.)

"Arabella! What did you do?"

By now Mr. Osgood stood in the doorway, knotting his tie. "What's the fuss?" he asked.

"She's cut her own bangs," Mrs. Osgood said. "Just look at the mess!"

The girl by the fire says, "Geez, it's just hair."

"Well," says her mother, "think of how she must look. And bangs are the worst. You can't fix that with another haircut. And you notice it every time you look at the person."

"So what happened?"

Well, it took some time for things to calm down. Arabella was crying by now and denying that she had done anything to her hair, because of course she hadn't. And then Rose walked toward Henrietta, who was standing at the closet, pretending to pick out a blouse for school.

"Do you know anything about this?" Rose demanded.

Of course, Henrietta denied it, but her face gave her away. On the long list of things that Henrietta was no good at, lying was near the top. Unfortunately, this fact had not made her any more honest.

Finally, with the nanny and her parents forming an accusatory semicircle around her, Henrietta cracked, began to cry, and admitted that she had cut her sister's bangs.

"My scissors!" her mother shouted. "So *that's* where my

scissors got to. Give them to me at once." And Henrietta was forced to march to her bed, head hanging in shame, and remove her secret treasure from beneath the mattress.

"What were you thinking?" her mother asked. "These are not a toy. And just look at your sister! Look at her. She looks ridiculous."

Arabella, who had gone to the mirror to study the damage, broke down. "I do!" she wailed. "I look ridiculous!" Then she threw herself on the bed, sobbing into her pillow.

"Oh dear," said Mr. Osgood, glancing at his watch and slipping out of the room, leaving his wife and the nanny to settle things. Mrs. Osgood and Rose huddled in the corner, deciding what to do while Henrietta began to plead with Arabella.

"It's not that bad," Henrietta insisted, rushing to her sister's side. "Arabella, really, it doesn't look that bad."

But Arabella waved her sister away, too angry to speak through her tears.

"Oh, don't be mad!" Henrietta begged. "I didn't mean it."

Henrietta looked stricken. Her regret was intense and immediate. She knew, of course, that she had gone too far and that Arabella had every right to be furious. Still, she couldn't stand the thought that the rift between them would now deepen. Their hearts, like magnets, once drawn together, would now press apart.

Rose eased Henrietta away from her sister's bed. Grasping her by the shoulders, she locked eyes with her.

"Why?" she asked.

"Why not?" Henrietta burst out. "Everything's always so perfect for her! Let her see how it feels for once."

"Your sister's never done anything to you!" Mrs. Osgood exclaimed.

"She's never done anything *for* me either," Henrietta said. And then the tears overtook her as well.

In the end, Arabella was allowed to stay home from school that morning, and Henrietta was sent off with a note for Mr. Stilton-Sterne.

> Dear Mr. Stilton-Sterne,
>
> Please excuse Henrietta for being late this morning. Sometime during the night she attacked her sister with a pair of sewing shears. Naturally, we are all quite shocked. Her poor sister is traumatized. And we won't even speak of the long-term damage to Arabella's appearance.
>
> Mrs. Osgood
>
> P.S. Please be sure Henrietta receives the standard punishments for tardy students.

Mr. Stilton-Sterne raised an eyebrow and said, "Henrietta, this is monstrous. What were you thinking? You are in serious trouble. Go take your seat."

. . .

Mrs. Osgood and Arabella seemed destined to spend the day weeping, until Rose (who was quite fashionable when not forced to wear her uniform) suggested a solution.

"Perhaps a hat," she said as she ruffled Arabella's bangs with her fingers. "Or even an especially nice scarf."

So Arabella and her mother set off for town to find some hats or scarves that would cover the crooked bangs. And as soon as Henrietta arrived home from school, she learned what her punishment would be. She knew that it was serious from the look on her father's face and the fact that he was home early, which had only happened once before (when he ate some bad fish).

The Osgoods had decided that Henrietta was to be sent away.

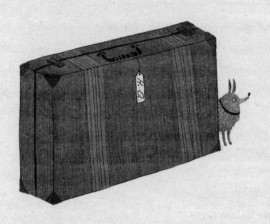

##  BANISHED

"She has to leave?" asks the girl by the fire, brushing cookie crumbs off her jumper. "That's a bit harsh, isn't it?"

"They thought it was best," the mother says.

"Where did she go?" asks the girl.

---

The girls had a great aunt, Priscilla Renfrew, who lived in a small neighboring town. She was a bit odd, but willing. So the arrangements fell into place. And that was that. They packed Henrietta's things, and her father loaded them up, and they left.

"What about school?" the girl asks.

"She wasn't allowed to go after that."

"Isn't that illegal?"

"Parents can do as they please," the mother says. "We have great power."

"Be serious. What about Henrietta?"

"Well, her life was very different for a time."

For now, picture her, her bags packed, tears streaming down her face. Henrietta tried to kiss her mother goodbye, but she just turned her face away.

"What about Arabella?"

As Henrietta was leaving, she looked back at the house, and Arabella was there in the bedroom window, waving good-bye. Henrietta couldn't tell at that distance, but she thought Arabella was crying too.

## PRISCILLA RENFREW

Imagine what a wretched ride it was for Mr. Osgood and Henrietta. Her loud sobbing was quite distracting to her father, who had had quite enough of both girls for one day.

"Listen," he said, trying to sound soothing. "This isn't the worst thing. The house is old, but it's roomy. And Aunt Priscilla is very interesting in her own way. You should really try to think of this as an adventure."

Henrietta hiccupped. "An adventure?" she asked.

"Yes. And blow your nose."

Just then they pulled up to the house.

"Go ahead," he urged her, giving her a little nudge. Henrietta walked, knees knocking, to the door.

She rang the bell and was met by silence, so she turned to ask her father what she should do, but he had already left her bags behind and was pulling out of the semicircular drive. Little puffs of dust swirled where he had been, and she heard him calling goodbye as he rounded the corner.

"Now what?" she thought.

She tried to ring the bell twice more, then settled down on the front stoop, head in her hands, for a good cry. Henrietta had been weeping rather loudly for several minutes when she caught sight of something floating down from the upstairs window. It was a fancy sheet of ivory-colored stationery with an elaborate interlocking P and R at the top. It said:

*The door is unlocked, you foolish girl.*
*Stop your silly crying and open it.*

*P. Renfrew*

"That isn't very friendly," says the girl.

"Well," says the mother, taking a sip of tea, "she wasn't a very friendly woman."

## ❧ SETTLING IN ☙

Henrietta opened the door and went inside. The place was
pitch-dark, even in the middle of the day, because all the curtains had been drawn. Aunt Priscilla Renfrew was just descending the stairs, dressed completely in black and carrying
a large black cat in her arms.

"Don't just stand there," she said to Henrietta. "Come
over here and introduce yourself properly."

"My name is Henrietta."

"I know your name. Aren't you going to curtsy or take my
hand?" Priscilla asked, tossing the cat to the floor.

The hand in question was wrinkled and covered with

twisty purplish veins and liver spots. Priscilla's fingernails were long and blood-red. On her right hand was an enormous emerald ring, as beautiful as the hand itself was ugly. Henrietta closed her eyes, held her breath, and gave the hand a quick shake.

"Very well," Priscilla said. "Take your things upstairs. First bedroom on the left is yours for now."

Henrietta struggled to get the suitcase upstairs. It was hugely heavy and bumped against every step.

"Quiet, if you please!" Priscilla shouted.

At this Henrietta startled and let go of the suitcase, which toppled down to the bottom stair and sprang open, so she had to stuff her skirts and kneesocks back inside and start the whole exhausting process over again from the beginning. When at last she reached the room, she shoved the suitcase inside, kicking it with her foot. The door squeaked. The room was cold and dark, but it had a large canopy bed in the center with two more black cats at the foot of it. They hissed as Henrietta entered.

"I hope she wasn't allergic to cats," the girl says.

"That was her only piece of luck," the mother tells her.

## ❧ DINNER IS SERVED ❧

Henrietta was unsure of what she should do. The room was uninviting, but the idea of going downstairs again was even more awful, so she opened her suitcase and started to unpack her things. It calmed her a bit to touch them, the familiar wool skirts and white cotton blouses with their rounded collars. Henrietta was bent over the suitcase when Priscilla appeared in the doorway.

"I have other ways to occupy you," she said.

Henrietta jumped. Then she screamed.

"What is the matter with you? You're worse than they said."

"I'm sorry," said Henrietta. "You startled me. That's all. What would you like me to do?"

Priscilla took her to the kitchen and told her to make soup. Henrietta protested that she didn't know how to cook, but Priscilla gave her a recipe and handed her a bowl of lumpy-looking vegetables and three packages wrapped in white paper.

"Follow the recipe," she said.

Henrietta looked around the room, examining each detail of her new surroundings. The cutting boards were covered with dark, watery stains, and the room was drafty. Bundles of dried leaves and slightly rusty pots swung from a wooden rack overhead. Henrietta had no idea where to begin. She felt utterly alone and hopeless and was standing stock-still with a blank look on her face when Priscilla stuck her head into the room a second time.

"Well, go ahead!" Priscilla urged from the doorway. "The soup isn't going to make itself!"

So Henrietta gathered her courage, grabbed a large knife, and started to chop up the meat in the first package. It seemed ordinary enough. The recipe called for butter and onions, so she sliced those too. But as they were sizzling in the pan, she realized that the other two white paper packages were still there. When Henrietta opened the next one, a small, wet, red-brown organ fell out into her hand. Henrietta shrieked. It looked like the heart of a small animal.

"And the third package?" asks the girl.

"Fish heads," says the mother. "Quite common in soups, really, but Henrietta didn't know that. She screamed again—just as loudly—when she saw them."

"This is too awful," says the girl.

"It's not that horrible, really. A lot of tasty things have odd ingredients, you know. Steak and kidney pie, for one."

"You know what I mean. She shouldn't even be there. She only made the one mistake. Cutting her sister's bangs."

"Sometimes the smallest missteps have unimagined consequences," the mother says.

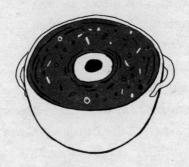

## NIGHT TERRORS

Believe it or not, Henrietta was not the only one suffering. Mr. and Mrs. Osgood thought that Arabella's life would return to normal as soon as her bangs grew back and her sister went away. Unfortunately, they had underestimated the depth of the attachment between their daughters. For as opposite as they were, Arabella and Henrietta were twins, and twins are connected in strange and mysterious ways that only another twin can really understand.

And so the very night that Henrietta left for Aunt Priscilla's, Arabella woke up screaming. The nanny had to rush to her bedside. It turned out that Arabella had had a terrible nightmare. It was something about a strange house, a woman in black, and an awful bowl of soup with an eye floating in it. She was crying so hard that it was difficult for the Osgoods to understand exactly what she was saying.

"She's cutting up a heart," she sobbed.

"Cutting out your heart? Oh my goodness no! You've had an awful nightmare."

"For the soup," Arabella insisted.

"She's not making any sense," Mrs. Osgood said to Rose. "Get the thermometer. I think she must have a fever."

"Perhaps we should call the doctor."

In the end, Arabella went back to sleep with a cool cloth on her forehead and a small light turned on at her bedside. Her mother slept beside her, in Henrietta's bed, thinking it would calm Arabella. But every hour or so, Arabella woke up with another terrible nightmare about cats sleeping on her bed or long red fingernails. No matter what her parents and Rose did, they couldn't seem to end the bad dreams for the night.

"I have two questions," the girl says.

"All right," the mother sighs.

"First, is that true about the connection between twins?"

"Of course. Why do you think they dress alike?"

"And another thing. Don't you think she acted like a baby by having her mother sleep with her?"

"Well, dear, only Mrs. Osgood and Arabella know the answer to that."

## 🌿 NOTES AND MESSAGES 🌿

The next morning, while Arabella was away at school, it suddenly dawned on Mrs. Osgood what had caused the dream in the first place.

"It's Priscilla," she said. "Somehow she's dreaming of Priscilla. Don't you see? The cats and the fingernails and that awful food Priscilla eats."

"That's impossible," Mr. Osgood said, without lowering the morning paper.

"It isn't impossible at all," said Mrs. Osgood. "It's the only thing that makes sense. I'd call her myself if she had a telephone. You have to go and speak to her. She's *your* aunt."

"And yours," said Mr. Osgood, "by marriage."

"Nevertheless," Mrs. Osgood said. "And do it right away. We can't spend another night like last night. Arabella needs her rest."

"But what will I say?" whined Mr. Osgood, who, truth be told, hated any kind of conflict.

"Do you want me to drive over there?" Mrs. Osgood asked, in a tone that suggested it was more of a threat than an offer of assistance.

"That's a lot of bother, dear. Don't trouble yourself. I'll send a telegram on the way to the office," Mr. Osgood said. "Oh! Look at the time! Have you seen my spectacles?"

"They're on top of your head," said Mrs. Osgood.

"So they are," said Mr. Osgood, reaching to locate them and giving his wife a small salute. "I'm off! Bye now."

And so that was settled. Mr. Osgood escaped his wife and avoided a long, painful conversation with his aunt. He sent a telegram to Aunt Priscilla that said:

ARABELLA HAVING BAD DREAMS STOP

"Stop what?" the girl asks her mother.

"That's how they sent a telegram," the mother explains. "The 'stop' is like a period."

"But that doesn't really tell her what to do," the girl says.

"I suppose they weren't exactly sure what Priscilla would do to make the dreams stop."

"What did she do?"

When Priscilla got the telegram, she had the same reaction as her nephew, Mr. Osgood. Priscilla didn't see how *she* was responsible for Arabella's nightmares. So she took out her stationery and a quill pen and wrote Mr. Osgood a letter.

> Osgood,
>
> Imagine my surprise at having my lunch interrupted by your odd telegram about Arabella and her nightmares. I cannot imagine what you think I can do to assist. If I am not mistaken, the child has two parents as well as a nanny. And I, you will recall, have already taken in her sister—who, by the way, is prone to fits of screaming and is so untrained that she cannot even follow a simple recipe!
>
> Yours,
> Priscilla

. . .

Priscilla licked the envelope and handed it to Henrietta. "Take this to the post office," she said, depositing some coins for postage in Henrietta's upturned palm.

"Where's that?"

Aunt Priscilla sighed and gave a long and confusing set of directions: up a hill, down a hill, past the bookshop, across from the pharmacy, and so on. Henrietta was sure that she would get lost, but she was afraid of making Aunt Priscilla angry if she asked for further instructions, so she set off.

It was a cloudy day, threatening rain, and Henrietta was cold. She should have worn a sweater, but she never remembered, and her mother and the nanny weren't there to tell her to wear one, so she went without and shivered. Her socks kept falling down and bunching in her shoes, and every few feet she would stop and bend over to pull them up. The wind whipped her hair into her eyes, and the strands stung like salt in a cut. Henrietta was tired and miserable and sure that she was lost. Most melancholy of all was the sight of her parents' names and her own address on the letter she carried. Soon their hands would open this envelope, touch this same paper. Henrietta could picture the letter resting in the wicker basket on the hall table where they kept the mail, and a wave of homesickness hit her as she walked through the unfamiliar village all alone.

## HENRIETTA FINDS A FRIEND

As she walked, Henrietta thought of all that had happened since that fateful moment when she cut her sister's bangs. Suddenly she realized that she should have written a letter of her own, apologizing and begging her parents for another chance. Finally she passed the bookstore and decided to stop to see if she could borrow a pencil.

The woman behind the counter had beautiful dark hair and a kind face, so Henrietta decided to test her luck and ask for the pencil, which the woman gladly gave her. The letter was sealed tight, so she wrote on the back of the envelope.

*I am very sorry. I would like to come home.*
                                    *H.*

"Would you like me to mail that for you?" the woman asked.

"That's okay," Henrietta said. "I'm on my way to the post office myself, except I don't know exactly where it is."

"Why, it's miles away. Why don't you leave it here? I'll give it to the postman when he comes by."

The woman was so kind and sympathetic that Henrietta felt tears forming in her eyes. It seemed a very long time since anyone had been nice to her.

"Had anyone ever been nice to her?" the girl asks her mother.

"Arabella," the mother answers. "Before their argument. But that must have already seemed a long time ago."

The woman, who was called Inez, took Henrietta to the back of the store and gave her a peppermint from a jar she kept on her desk. Soon Henrietta was telling her the whole story about cutting Arabella's hair and how it had led to her being sent away.

"And this is only the second day," she sobbed. "And already I want to go home, but I know they'll never take me back."

"Perhaps they just wanted to teach you a lesson," Inez said. "When they hear how unhappy you are, surely they won't make you stay."

"But I think they will," Henrietta sobbed.

"And she's right, isn't she?" the girl asks her mother.

"Just let the story unfold," the mother advises.

Inez fixed Henrietta a cup of tea and told her to make herself at home in the shop.

"I should go," Henrietta said.

"No need to rush," Inez answered her, smiling. "Have your tea and look around a bit. A book can be a good friend on a cold, blustery day."

Henrietta sipped the tea, which tasted like lemons and honey. Then she tiptoed out into the store and began to look at the books. Inside each one was a whole world. The best had drawings as well as stories: horses and castles and dark, mysterious woods. The bell above the door would ring sometimes, and someone would buy a magazine or pick up a book they had ordered for someone's birthday. Henrietta ignored them, curled up in a soft chair, and read. She stayed so long that soon it was time for the shop to close. It was raining by now, and Inez offered to take Henrietta back to Aunt Priscilla's house. She also gave Henrietta two things.

"Can you guess what they were?" the mother asks.

"A pile of gold," the girl says.

"Not likely," says the mother. "Though Inez was wearing some lovely gold earrings."

"Another peppermint."

"One piece of candy is more than enough," says the mother.

Inez gave Henrietta a book of stories and, best of all, a promise that if she did not return home and if Aunt Priscilla allowed it, Henrietta could work in the shop on Thursday afternoons. So Henrietta rode with Inez back to Aunt Priscilla's house in the rain, uphill and downhill, daydreaming the whole way. When they arrived, Henrietta thanked Inez for her kindness. Then she tucked the book beneath her waistband, wrapping her arms around it. Henrietta most definitely did not want to have to explain where she had been, though she needn't have worried, as Priscilla seemed to have disappeared.

That night, Henrietta dreamed she was reading the book of stories in the shop, next to a crackling fire. And far away, in her bed, Arabella dreamed the same dream and smiled.

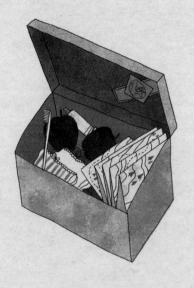

## ARABELLA PLANS A RESCUE

Although Mr. and Mrs. Osgood were as happy as could be now that Henrietta was out of the house, Arabella was sad. She missed her sister's company in the evenings, missed their games. This surprised her because before Henrietta left, there were times when Arabella hadn't really paid much attention to her sister, times when Henrietta was, more or less, just a lump underneath the covers in the opposite bed at night. But once Henrietta left, the house was too quiet. Arabella began to miss her sister and worry about her. On the playground at school, her circle of friends speculated about Henrietta and what her life was like.

"Is she a servant girl?" they would ask.

"Does she sleep by the fire like Cinderella?"

"I don't know," Arabella was forced to answer. But the truth was that ever since her own nightmares began, Arabella had suspected that her sister's new life wasn't very nice.

"Maybe she's in danger," Arabella's friend Lacey said.

But this seemed improbable until the afternoon when Arabella noticed a pile of mail on the hall table and flipped through it, which she was not supposed to do. She saw the letter from Aunt Priscilla, and she saw the note of apology that Henrietta had written across the back. Arabella was sure that when her parents saw it, they would regret their decision and bring Henrietta home. Then things would be back to normal, and she could sleep better at night with Henrietta in the next bed to whisper to in the dark.

At dinner that night, Mrs. Osgood asked her husband, "Anything interesting come in the post?"

Mr. Osgood shook his head. "Nothing much. Letter from Priscilla, full of complaints."

"Just like her," said Mrs. Osgood. "What does she want?"

"It's not her so much," said Mr. Osgood. "It's Henrietta herself. Wants to come home."

"Can she?" asked Arabella. "Please?"

"Oh, I don't think so," said Mrs. Osgood.

"Right. Best leave things as they are," agreed Mr. Osgood.

And when the girls at school asked her if her sister was ever coming home, Arabella had to say that she was not. And then, for some reason, perhaps because she felt sad or perhaps just as much because their pity gave her a warm feeling of pleasure, Arabella's eyes welled with tears, just as her sister's had that day in the shop. This got them all excited, and they patted her hair and handed her handkerchiefs and asked her not to cry.

"Why don't you go and visit her?" Lacey suggested.

"My parents would never let me."

They agreed that it was sad, and Lacey gave Arabella a chocolate to make her feel better. Then the bell rang, and they had to go back to class. But Arabella was taken with what they had said. She decided that she should find a way to visit Henrietta whether her parents wanted her to or not. And she started to lay her plan. In a box underneath her bed, she began to store up what she thought she would need: allowance money she had saved and clean underwear and a map she snuck out of her father's study and a couple of apples she could eat if she got hungry along the way. She even snuck Priscilla's letter from the basket on the hall table and copied Priscilla's address on a small slip of paper. Arabella was ready, but she knew that sneaking away might prove difficult. Leaving before school was impossible because Rose kept a close eye on her. And once she got to school, there was no way of doing anything without Mr. Stilton-Sterne noticing.

Arabella confided in her friends, and they discussed the problem endlessly. They loved the drama of it. You couldn't blame them, really—so little happened in their young lives. But soon Arabella's plans to run away were the talk of the playground. The girls even made up a jump-rope rhyme:

*She escapes after dark*
*Takes a walk*
*Through the park*
*Mother cries, father frowns*
*She is miles out of town*
*One, two, three, four . . .*

And the boys were prepared to perform the rescue themselves if the girls proved too timid.

"I can find your sister for you," Brendan Crowhurst bragged. "If you're too scared to go."

"She's not too scared," Lacey said. "She's just waiting for the right time."

As it turned out, the right time presented itself that very afternoon when Mr. Stilton-Sterne announced that he would be away the next day and the class would have a substitute teacher.

"I've got it!" Arabella shouted at recess. "When the other teacher calls my name, you just tell her I got moved to another class."

"That won't work," Lacey said. "She'll check, and we'll get caught."

"Look," said Brendan, butting into the conversation as usual, "when she calls Arabella's name, somebody just says, 'Here.' She won't know any of us. It's easy to fool a substitute."

They had to agree that Brendan had a point. And his tone did not exactly encourage protest. After that, the deal seemed sealed. Everyone was in on it. For once, they were all looking forward to school the next morning.

## A STRANGE DISCOVERY

Henrietta, of course, had no idea what Arabella was planning. For her, each day dragged on with no real prospect that her situation would ever change. Without school to occupy her, Henrietta had many empty hours to fill. Even the countless chores Priscilla gave her did not seem to last long enough.

Priscilla was not much of a conversationalist. When she was not devouring one of the hideous soups or stews that sustained her, she could be found in front of the fire reading, napping, or murmuring to one of her cats. In fact, she seemed to have more to say to them than she did to Henrietta.

Left to her own devices, Henrietta began to quietly explore the second story of the house. She examined the books on

Priscilla's shelves, which were mostly accounts of great wars or long biographies of elderly gentlemen Henrietta couldn't quite identify, though their faces all seemed vaguely familiar. Finally she opened the door to a large closet in the wide hallway. Henrietta knew she was snooping, but her curiosity got the better of her. Inside the closet's dim interior were piles of shiny fabric and stacks of small magazines and photographs. One especially intriguing gold-and-lace bundle was stowed on the top shelf. Henrietta stood on her tiptoes and leaned forward as far as she could, stretching toward her prize.

That was when the whole thing came tumbling down: the top shelf (only loosely attached under the best of circumstances) tipped forward, and a gold dress, a pile of fabric, photographs, feather boas, and lace rained down on Henrietta. She took a small step backward, twisted her ankle, and landed with a thud on the hallway floor. The commotion brought Priscilla from her comfortable seat by the fire up into the drafty hallway.

"Oh no!" she said. "My things! What have you done to my things?!"

Henrietta, still in shock, just blinked at her from the floor, a feather boa around her neck and another in her hair. She looked as dazed and helpless as a baby chick.

"I was just—" she started.

"Going through my closet," Priscilla finished for her. "I can see that."

Priscilla rushed to pick up the gold dress, caressing the brilliant material as if it were one of her beloved cats.

"Here," Henrietta said, attempting to stand. "Let me help you."

It was then she realized what she had done to her ankle, which was already beginning to swell. Priscilla sighed, dragged a small wooden chair out of her bedroom, and helped Henrietta onto it; then she went to get ice while Henrietta, humiliated and in pain, surveyed the mess at her feet.

When Priscilla returned, Henrietta asked, "What is all this?"

"My past," Priscilla said wistfully.

"What do you mean?"

"Haven't your parents told you anything about me?" she asked. "Who I am? Who I was?"

"No," Henrietta said softly, as ashamed of her ignorance as of the fallen papers and clothes at her feet.

"See for yourself, then," Priscilla said, handing her a small booklet.

Henrietta studied the drawing on the cover. It was a lovely young woman wearing the gold dress that Priscilla

was now folding. Her hair was in an elaborate bun, jewels hung around her neck, and she had vivid green eyes.

"Is this. . ."—Henrietta slowly realized it as she spoke— ". . . you?"

"Who else would it be?" Priscilla asked.

"But you look so different," Henrietta blurted.

Priscilla was looking at the cover now herself.

"It was a long time ago," she said.

"Tell me about it," Henrietta said. "Please."

And so they stayed there for a time in the upstairs hallway while the ice melted against Henrietta's wounded ankle, and Priscilla described her glory days on the stage: her favorite plays, her favorite roles, the thrill of looking out at the audience's faces, lifted expectantly toward the stage.

"Were you famous?" Henrietta asked.

"For a time," Priscilla said, "I had my admirers."

And she gazed down at her emerald ring.

"No wonder they gave you jewels. You were so beautiful," Henrietta said. "Arabella is too. Not like me."

"What are you talking about?" Priscilla said. "All the women in our family are beauties."

"Not me," said Henrietta.

"Nonsense," Priscilla insisted. "It's a matter of confidence. People will believe what you want them to believe. Every good actor knows that. Here," she said, rearranging the boa around Henrietta's neck and perching a large hat on her head. Then she stepped to her room, and when she returned, she handed Henrietta a mirror.

"It's important," she told Henrietta, "to see yourself as you really are."

Then Priscilla began collecting her treasures and storing them in the dark closet.

"What a disaster," she muttered to herself as Henrietta studied her face in the mirror, turning her head this way and that.

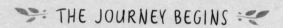 THE JOURNEY BEGINS

As Henrietta was gaining a bit of confidence for the first time, Arabella was losing hers. The truth was that Arabella was a little afraid of sneaking off. She had heard her mother talking about Aunt Priscilla, and some of the things she said were scary. And despite the map, Arabella wasn't at all sure she would know the way. All through dinner she kept thinking up little excuses for not leaving that she could use at school the next morning. She could say that it looked too much like rain, or that she hadn't had a chance to pack. If nothing else worked, she could fall back on the most time-honored and impossible-to-prove excuse of all: she could tell them she had a terrible stomachache. If Brendan protested, and he probably would, Arabella knew she could whip up some fake tears, and the girls would circle around her until the boys lost interest and backed off.

Arabella was so convinced she could get out of leaving that she began to relax and enjoy dessert. (It was her favorite: chocolate silk pie.) But that night, something happened that convinced her she had to leave after all. Arabella had a dream that she was sleeping in a cold, drafty room in a strange, dark bed. Black cats kept wandering in and out, and she was freezing and hungry. Arabella tossed and turned in her bed until she woke herself up.

"That room is real!" she whispered out loud to herself. "That's the room Henrietta has to sleep in. How awful!"

Arabella looked over at the empty bed beside her, and her eyes filled with real tears as she remembered the day Henrietta was sent away. "She's never done anything *for* me either!" Henrietta had shouted that day. And right then and there, in the deep dark middle of the night, Arabella resolved to take to the road and find her sister.

"Wasn't she frightened?" asks the girl.

"Of course," says the mother. "But sometimes it's the most frightening thing that most needs doing."

"But how did she know where to go?" the girl asks her mother.

"That's the thing. She really didn't."

Arabella located the town on the map and knew that it was north of where she lived. Then she remembered the little signs that her teacher had hung on the walls at school to help them learn about directions.

"Never eat soggy worms," the girl says.

"I beg your pardon?"

"That's how you remember it. The directions. Never eat soggy worms."

"Oh. I get it," the mother says.

So the next morning, Arabella stood in front of the school, watching as her nanny waved goodbye and headed back toward home. Then Arabella imagined herself inside her classroom, facing the side where they kept the class gerbils, Mike and Pat. She took a deep breath, turned north, and started out.

## ✤ SOME HELP ALONG THE WAY ✤

At first she was walking through her own neighborhood, then another near her school, then out on a country lane, and across a hill covered with small stones and purple heather. She saw goats and small houses and lost track of the road. Finally she saw a crooked little old man who seemed to be taking care of the goats, and she decided she would ask him if she was going in the right direction.

"Let me think," he said. He stroked his stubbly chin. "Seems to me like you *are* going north, but hadn't you better stick to the road? You'll be stepping in cow pies this way."

"Where is the road?" Arabella asked.

The old man told her to walk with him a bit, and he

would get her squared away. She hesitated at first because she had been given all the usual and correct warnings about talking to strangers. But the man seemed nice, and Arabella reasoned that as she was already in the next town over, anyone she met was likely to be a stranger. So Arabella walked beside the old man for a time.

"What brings you this way?" he asked.

Arabella stopped for a minute and thought about how best to describe it. It seemed silly to say that her sister had attacked her bangs and had been sent away and was now trapped in a strange room with a dusty old bed and dozens of dark creepy cats.

"My sister's in trouble," she said instead. "And she needs my help. I'm trying to find my way to her."

"Maybe I can help," the man said.

Arabella took the map out of her book bag and showed him where she was going.

He traced the route she should follow with one long, crooked finger; then he said, "I think we've got you sorted. Healthy walk, but you'll be there in a bit."

"I hope so," Arabella said. "I have to get to her no matter how long it takes. Henrietta doesn't even want to be with Aunt Priscilla—"

"Priscilla?" the old man asked as a strange look came over his face. "Tell me, what's her last name?"

"Renfrew," Arabella said.

"Oh my," the man said slowly.

And then it all came out.

## ❧ PRISCILLA'S PAST ❧

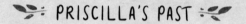

"He knows her?" the girl asks her mother.

"That's what I'm getting to."

It seems he knew Priscilla from his youth, when they were both aspiring young actors. He was one of the many taken by her beauty and talent on the stage.

"But," he told Arabella, "there was something unnatural about it. The way she seemed to change for every part. It was like she became another person every time, like she cast a spell."

"You see!" the girl shouts. "He's saying she's a witch."

"Well," says the mother, "she certainly had mysterious powers."

The old man described how Priscilla's was always the most amazing performance in any play.

"Nobody ever saw her backstage putting on her makeup. She never seemed to be in the wings waiting to go on. When it was time, she just appeared onstage looking so much like the character that it confused the rest of us. The other actors."

Arabella stood completely still, engrossed in the story.

"You would almost forget your own lines, staring at her face," the old man went on. "The only way you ever knew it was her was by her eyes. Those amazing green eyes."

He said that every actor in the troupe was in love with her. And a funny, glazed look came over his face.

"This must be a different Priscilla," Arabella said. "I've seen pictures of her, and she's as ugly as . . ."

"As a witch!" the girl shouts at her mother.

". . . can be. As ugly as can be. *That's* what Arabella said."

"No," the old man said. "There's no mistake. There's only one Priscilla Renfrew. Of course, she's gotten older, like all of us. She wouldn't look the same now, I expect. But no one knows for sure. Nobody's seen her for years."

"Well, I'm about to," said Arabella. And she thanked him for his help. He gave her a leg up so she could climb a fence and get back on the road. And he pointed the way and wished her good luck. Then he offered her some water from the pouch he had slung over his shoulder, but she politely refused. And then Arabella was on her way again.

## THE RUNAWAY

Of course, at home it was quite a scene come three forty-five when Arabella failed to appear. Rose rushed in and said she couldn't find Arabella at school.

"What?!" yelled Mrs. Osgood, putting her art supplies away so quickly that she ruined a perfectly good new paintbrush. Then she called her husband and told him to meet her at the school. And she hurried off to find the principal, who was just leaving for the day. Mrs. Osgood charged into his office, demanding to know if he had seen Arabella.

"Let's see if she's still in class," Principal Rothbottom said, leading Mrs. Osgood toward Arabella's classroom. They arrived just as the substitute teacher, Miss Brittlewhite, was locking the door.

"Have you seen the Osgood girl?" he asked her.

"She has a name!" Mrs. Osgood said.

But Principal Rothbottom was too busy quizzing Miss Brittlewhite to notice how upset Mrs. Osgood was.

"I'm asking you a question. Did Della report for school today?"

"Arabella!" Mrs. Osgood exclaimed. "Her name is Arabella!"

"Which one is she?" Miss Brittlewhite asked.

"This is outrageous!" shouted Mrs. Osgood.

"Well, there are dozens of children; I get them confused," Miss Brittlewhite admitted. "But I had all the children who were on the list. I took attendance. I swear I did."

And, of course, she had. But, just as they had planned yesterday on the playground, another girl answered for Arabella, and Miss Brittlewhite never knew the difference.

Principal Rothbottom turned to Arabella's mother. "Mrs. Osgood," he said, "I assure you we will do all we can to help you find your daughter."

"I should hope you would!" she snapped.

And so on. It was one of those fights that grown-ups have without any shouting. It was full of sighing and nasty looks. In the middle of it all, Mr. Osgood arrived and listened as his wife and the principal explained that Arabella was missing.

"I think the point, my dear, is that it's time to contact the authorities," Mr. Osgood told his wife. "We need to institute a search."

"I'm afraid I agree," said Principal Rothbottom.

Mrs. Osgood turned pale. She began to imagine bloodhounds and policemen slopping through the woods and shallow streams looking for Arabella. Mrs. Osgood started to panic. Mr. Osgood took his wife home and called the doctor to come over and give her a shot.

"A shot?" the girl asks her mother. "What for?"

"Well, to help her calm down. Imagine how upset she must be. Her daughter is missing."

"A shot doesn't help you calm down," the girl says. "Just seeing the needle is scary."

"A certain kind of shot can help you calm down."

"Like the kind they blow out of a dart gun to take down an elephant?"

"Of course not! Where do you get these things?" the mother asks.

Mr. Osgood took his wife home, and their house was full of people: Dr. Waverly tending to Mrs. Osgood; and the police, asking questions; and the neighbors, who said they were worried but who also, as anyone knows, were just being nosy.

Principal Rothbottom, true to his word, stopped by later to see if there was anything the school could do to help.

"What did they do?" the girl asks. "To find her?"

"Well, the first thing they did was to call her friend Lacey to see if she knew anything."

"What did she say?" asks the girl.

"Nothing. Brendan Crowhurst had made them all swear to secrecy."

"You mean she was more afraid of a bully than the police?"

"Well, police and teachers don't rule the playground, I'm afraid," the mother says. "Brendan's word was law there. Besides, Lacey wanted Arabella to reach her sister."

"Good point," says the girl. "And there's never any telling how things will turn out once you let grown-ups interfere."

"Well, quite a few were already involved in the search for Arabella."

Principal Rothbottom promised to have Mr. Northington, the assistant principal, question the children at school the next morning. It would give Northington something useful to do instead of frittering away the day, settling minor playground disputes or mooning over the librarian.

And, as Mrs. Osgood suspected, the police sent out dogs. They asked Mr. Osgood, who asked Rose, for a piece of Arabella's clothing, so the dogs could get her scent. Then they started off. Mr. Osgood and the principal promised to let Mrs. Osgood know as soon as they found out anything about what had happened to Arabella.

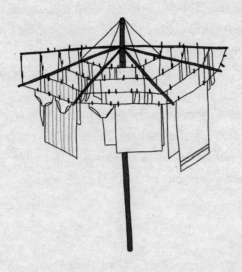

## ⚛ A KIND BUT CURIOUS STRANGER ⚛

"What *had* happened to Arabella?" the girl asks.

"Well, actually, it wasn't scary at all," the mother says. "At least not at first."

Arabella, who had stopped to pet a small dog, met a woman who was out in her yard, hanging up laundry.

"Are you lost?" the woman asked.

Although Arabella had done her best to read the map and follow the route the old man had outlined for her, she suspected she probably *was* lost. She was afraid to admit this, however, in case the woman might decide she should call for help.

So she said, "I'm fine. I'm just on my way to my aunt's house."

The bad part was that the woman seemed suspicious and kept asking a lot of questions. The good part was that she asked the questions in a warm kitchen at a table while she fed Arabella a delicious bowl of vegetable soup.

"Vegetable soup is not delicious," the girl says. "Chocolate cake is delicious."

"Chocolate cake is not a meal."

"Why are you so worried about what she's eating?" the girl asks. "Isn't the real point that she just talked to a complete stranger for the **second** time and went inside her house?"

"Good point," says the mother. "It's nice to know you're such a sensible child."

As Arabella ate her soup, the woman studied her.

"That's an interesting hairstyle you have," she said.

"Thanks," said Arabella. "My sister cut my bangs for me."

Arabella, who had pulled off her now-customary

headscarf, was surprised by the compliment. Yet, as the woman began to question her further, pleasure turned to nervousness.

"What did you say your aunt's name was?" asked the woman.

"Worthington," Arabella said. "Sarah Worthington."

That's right. Arabella told a lie. But what's even worse is that the name she selected actually belonged to her Sunday-school teacher. It may be hard to imagine nearly perfect Arabella making up a fib, but the fact was that the journey was already beginning to change her. Her shoes were dusty; her white anklets were smudged with dirt. And now she had told a lie. Arabella knew it was wrong to lie, but she also felt certain somehow that the woman meant to tell on her. She would call the Osgoods and tell them their daughter was here; it was the only thing that could happen next in the sparkling clean kitchen of such a sweet and responsible woman. Arabella sensed it, and she felt forced to lie if she wanted to keep walking long enough to find Henrietta.

"What time is she expecting you?" the woman asked next.

"Could I have some more water?" Arabella asked.

She had only hoped to change the subject, but the truth was that Arabella was beginning to panic. As the woman turned to fill Arabella's water glass, Arabella dashed out the door, leaving the woman to call out after her, "Wait! Don't go!"

Although Arabella was now off on a big adventure, Henrietta's life at Aunt Priscilla's house had settled into a routine. Each night she had to make kidney pie or fish-head stew.

"Each night? They ate horrible things like that every single night?"

"Well," says the mother, "children always complain that they're eating the same things all the time. Perhaps Aunt Priscilla just decided not to bother trying to vary the menu."

Of course, Henrietta never could force herself to take more than a few bites of these dinners, and even then she had to close her eyes and hold her breath to get the food down. Afterward she brushed her tongue with her toothbrush until it hurt. And the rest of the day, Aunt Priscilla kept her busy with odd jobs: catching spiders and teaching them to sing . . .

"What?"

"Well," the mother says, "I said they were odd jobs."

One morning they decided to name Aunt Priscilla's cats.

"They don't have names?" the girl asks.

"Apparently not."

When Henrietta realized that Priscilla was calling them "the gray one" or "the one with the white paws," she asked if they could name them.

"What for?" Priscilla asked.

"That's what people do with pets," Henrietta explained. "We could do it together. I'll start.

"Let's call that one Oatmeal."

"Oatmeal?" asks the girl.

"They were eating breakfast at the time."

Then Henrietta dubbed another cat Lulu, and Aunt Priscilla began to call a third Professor Wiggles. It took them the better part of the morning to name them all. In fact, they only stopped when it was time for Henrietta to go and help Inez. She had gotten Aunt Priscilla to agree that she could work in the bookshop. Of course, she would not be allowed to keep the money she earned, and she had to promise not to say anything about her life with Aunt Priscilla.

"This town is full of gossips," said Aunt Priscilla. "That's why I so seldom go out."

"She never goes out," says the girl to her mother.

"Exactly."

"You'd better get going or you'll be late," said Aunt Priscilla. "Come along, Professor Wiggles," she added, scooping up the cat and wandering toward the bookcase.

· · ·

Henrietta rushed off to her appointment with Inez. The bookshop was just as lovely as she remembered, and Henrietta was very happy there. She dusted the shelves and learned to work the cash register.

"There you are," she said as she counted out change into the hand of an older gentleman who had just bought a book of poetry for his wife.

"Well done," said Inez once the man had left. "You're a natural. I should have hired you years ago."

"You didn't know me years ago," said Henrietta.

"Excellent point. And entirely my loss. I plan to make up for it by getting to know all about you right now. What's your favorite color?"

"Purple," said Henrietta without hesitation.

"Lucky number?"

"Ten."

"Favorite pet?"

"I only have the one. Had the one. Muffin."

"No, no, none of that," said Inez when Henrietta began to frown. "You'll be home with Muffin soon enough. Today I have you all to myself."

Inez was good company. Sometimes when business slowed down, she even read stories from a huge book of fairy tales. And they were all about the usual fairy-tale things of girls trapped in towers or lost in forests, but everything always turned out right in the end. In fact, the girls always ended up happily married and ruling a small kingdom of their very own and never eating fish stew or kidney pie ever again. Just hearing the stories gave Henrietta hope that her own situation might change, somehow, for the better.

"How's that going to happen?" the girl asks. "Princes don't walk into a bookshop."

"You never know," the mother says. "Everyone needs something to read."

## ﾐ A GIANT NAMED GUS ﾐ

The job in Inez's store wasn't the only thing improving Henrietta's mood. Henrietta had a feeling that one day soon Arabella would be with her. And in the black bed, with cat whiskers tickling her cheek, Henrietta had a dream about her sister. The dream seemed more real to Henrietta than her waking life. She saw Arabella studying a map and slipping it into a secret box beneath her bed.

"That's amazing!" says the girl.

"It was," agrees the mother.

And soon Arabella had an amazing experience of her own. She met a giant named Gus.

"Oh, now you've gone too far!" says the girl. "If there can't be witches in the story, there can't be any giants."

"There could be witches, or wiccans, or whatever," the mother says. "There just don't happen to be. This is a true story from real life. I can't make up what didn't happen."

The girl frowns at her mother. "There are no giants in real life."

"Of course there are," says the mother. "It's an issue with the pituitary gland. You could look it up if you like. Or ask your teacher."

"So she met a giant?" asks the girl. "A real giant?"

"She did indeed," says the mother. "Only Arabella didn't realize at first that Gus was a giant because when she first happened upon him, Gus was lying down in the shade under a tree, reading a book with a canning jar of iced tea by his side. He looked tall, of course, but not as enormous as he did standing up."

"Did he say 'Fee Fi Fo Fum' and all that?"

"No. That story's already been told."

Gus liked to spend as much time outdoors as possible. His parents, who were of average height, had designed their house to accommodate their son's expanding frame. But they did not know at the time that Gus would grow so fond of trees and flowers, or that he would so often need to escape their harsh words and disappointment about their lives. The house felt cramped for Gus. And, although Arabella didn't know it, Gus's family blamed his height on none other than Priscilla Renfrew. They claimed she had put some sort of curse on Gus.

It started before Gus was even born. His parents went to see Priscilla in a play when they were dating. They were young and in love and much more interested in each other than they were in the play. And during the performance they started to whisper secrets and giggle. They were sitting in the front row, and their commotion seemed to throw Priscilla off. She stumbled over a few of her lines, and that was not like her at all. Afterward, as they were leaving the theater, Priscilla grabbed Gus's father by the sleeve.

"You'll pay for what you did to me today," she told him. She didn't say how, and she didn't say when, but she threatened them. Gus's father laughed in her face, and his mother wasn't worried either—not until the day, years later, when she found out she was pregnant with Gus. Then she remembered about Priscilla. She could still imagine Priscilla in front of them going on about how they would be sorry for what they had done. And suddenly she was terrified at the thought of what Priscilla might do to spoil their happiness.

For the rest of the pregnancy, she was afraid that something would be wrong with the baby. And, of course, they eventually found out that something was.

"But he's just different," the girl says. "Just tall. He could still live a perfectly good life."

"Well, yes," says the mother. "But being a giant is a terrible strain on your heart. Most of them die young."

"How sad!"

But Arabella didn't know any of this when she came upon Gus reading under the tree. She just saw his foot at first, his very large, bare foot lying there in the grass. Then her eyes traveled all the way up to his head, partially hidden by a copy of *A Gardener's Guide to Wildflowers*, which was one of his favorite books. The problem was that Arabella's own feet kept moving along with her eyes, and she was so shocked by what she was seeing that she tripped over Gus's foot, and he had to help her up. In a very deep voice, he asked if she was all right.

Then he asked, "You're afraid of me, aren't you?"

"Of course not," Arabella answered.

"Yes, you are," Gus insisted.

"Should I be?" Arabella asked.

"No, not at all. I'm sorry," Gus said. "I must be making a

terrible first impression. It's just that, you know, I get that a lot."

"What?"

"Abject terror. Trembling."

"Really?"

"No. I guess I'm exaggerating. But people are shocked sometimes. They tend to stare or say something stupid. They think I'm a lot older and much scarier than I really am."

"How old are you?" Arabella asked.

"I'm eleven. And not at all scary, in case you were going to ask."

"People get the wrong idea about me too," Arabella said. "Just because I'm blond . . ."

"And pretty," Gus added.

"Thank you," Arabella said with a blush. "Well, people talk to me like I'm dense."

"How annoying," Gus said.

"And I happen to be a straight-A student," Arabella told him.

Then, to Arabella's embarrassment, her stomach growled. Loudly.

Gus began to laugh, not unkindly, and that made Arabella laugh too.

"I'm terribly sorry," said Gus. "Where are my manners? My name is Gus."

"Arabella," she said, holding out her hand.

"You must be hungry, Arabella. Let's go inside. It's almost time for dinner, and you can meet my parents."

As they neared the house, Arabella could hear some boisterous singing.

"That's my mother," Gus said with an apologetic smile. "She likes opera."

"Oh," said Arabella. She felt she probably should have said more, offered some compliment, but it sounded like a cat whose tail had been pulled, and she doubted her ability to seem sincere.

"It's nice that she has a hobby," Arabella said after a long pause.

As they entered the house, Gus's mother was standing on a low stool in front of the sink. Her eyes were squeezed shut, her head thrown back. One arm was stretched forward, and the other was thrown across her substantial chest as she reached for a final high note. She opened her eyes when she heard them come in.

"Oh my!" she said, stumbling down off the stool. "Who do we have here?"

"This is Arabella," Gus said. "My new friend. I thought she might stay for dinner."

"Delightful! We're having pasta."

"She thinks we're in Italy," Gus whispered. "Let me show you the house."

Soon Gus's father joined them for the tour. The house was amazing, with high ceilings and large windows. Arabella told them right away how much she liked it.

"We designed it special," Gus's father said proudly. "Once we knew how big our boy would be."

"Sit down," his mother said. "Let's have something to eat."

She was an excellent cook and served the pasta with a wonderful salad and a lemony iced tea that Gus kept drinking from his canning jar. As they ate, they started discussing Arabella's journey. She felt so relaxed that eventually Arabella admitted she was on her way to see her sister.

"My parents sent her away," she explained. "To stay with my father's aunt. But I keep having terrible dreams, and I think she isn't happy. Maybe not even safe. So I have to go and find her."

"We dream all sorts of strange things, dear," said Gus's mother. "I'm sure she's fine. I bet she's doing something really lovely right this minute. Like eating an orange or having a nice nap."

But once Arabella started to give them details about her dreams, Gus and his family had to admit that the situation did sound dire.

"Aren't you afraid to go there?" asked Gus's father.

"Hush, Quentin. No need to frighten the girl, is there? Honestly, sometimes you don't have the sense—"

"If you would kindly let me finish *for a change*. I simply think—" said Gus's father.

"That's the whole trouble," his mother interrupted. "You don't stop to think."

"Let's go outside," whispered Gus. He was always embarrassed when his parents started to quarrel, and he knew from experience that once they started, it would go on for a while and could get very loud.

"Sorry about that," Gus said as they stood outside together in the green grass.

"Don't be silly," Arabella told him. "It isn't your fault."

But she found somehow that she couldn't quite look at him now.

"Perhaps I'd better be going," she said.

"I wish you could stay," Gus said. "We never get visitors, and it's been so interesting talking to you."

Arabella smiled at him. Inside, the loud voices continued.

"Well," Gus said at last, "perhaps you're right. I hate to send you off alone, though; do you want me to come with you?"

Now, the truth was that Arabella did want Gus to come along, but she was trying to be practical. Despite sharing her story with Gus and his family, she was still planning to keep a low profile—as behooves a runaway. And it isn't easy to be inconspicuous when you're traveling with a giant.

"Thank you," said Arabella, "but I think I should go alone. I'll be all right."

"Let me give you something," said Gus.

"He's going to give her a rabbit's foot," says the girl. "For luck."

"I've never understood why a rabbit's foot is good luck. It certainly wasn't lucky for the rabbit."

"Mother! Get on with the story."

"I was just going to say that Gus gave her a silver whistle."

"Here," said Gus as he slid the whistle onto a blue ribbon and tied it around Arabella's neck. "For safety. In case you get lost."

"I'm not sure if I should be more afraid of getting lost or of being found," Arabella said, and smiled. "But thank you."

They could still hear Gus's parents yelling at one another and throwing pots and pans around the kitchen.

Arabella gave Gus a sympathetic look. "Will you be all right?" she asked.

"Sure," he said. "This happens a lot."

So Arabella stood on her tiptoes; she grabbed Gus's hand and squeezed it.

"Goodbye, my friend," she whispered.

She realized now that Henrietta wasn't the only one who didn't have a very nice place to live. But she had a mission. And she decided to get on with it.

## ⁓ NIGHT FALLS ⁓

After she left Gus, Arabella soon reached a small, unfamiliar town. It was evening now, and the lights were beginning to come on in the houses. Through the windows she could see people settling in for the night: washing up dishes or stooping to pet a dog. Looking at them from the damp sidewalk was impossibly sad. A part of her began to wish that someone along the way had called her parents. Perhaps the woman who questioned her so closely at lunchtime had telephoned the police by now, and any minute her parents would be coming to collect her. That was what Arabella hoped. The truth was that Arabella was out in the wide world on her own. However much that kindly woman may have worried initially, she never did notify the authorities.

"So nobody is going to help her?" asks the girl.

"That's not what I said. As you recall, the police were already at the Osgoods' house."

Mrs. Osgood rested—propped up on pillows in her blue satin robe—on a couch in the center of the living room as the police explained that it was quite possible Arabella hadn't run away at all but had been snatched.

"What can we do?" Mrs. Osgood asked.

"Try not to worry, ma'am," said the chief of police. "My men are searching for her now with the dogs."

Mrs. Osgood gasped loudly at this.

"I'll post guards around the house. I'd expect a call, or a note, fairly soon if this is a kidnapping."

"I think I'm going to faint," said Mrs. Osgood.

"There must be something else we can do," Mr. Osgood exclaimed, but the police insisted they were doing all they could, and there was nothing left to do but wait.

Eventually, Mrs. Osgood fell asleep, with Muffin snoring softly on her lap. And Mr. Osgood paced the floor, worrying about Arabella. He was surprised to find himself thinking too of Henrietta. How was it possible that, without really meaning to, he had somehow given one girl away and lost the other? He stared out of the front window into the rainy night, where his own worried reflection hovered like a ghost.

"But they are going to find her, aren't they?" the girl asks.

"They were trying very hard," says the mother.

As the Osgoods waited, the search party was spreading out across the town. Police in yellow rain slickers followed the lead of their trained dogs. Parents and neighbors trailed along beside them, calling Arabella's name and aiming their flashlight beams into the darkness.

## ❧ A MODEST PROPOSAL ❧

While most of the town was in an uproar over Arabella's disappearance, there were a few people who were still blissfully unaware of what had transpired. Two of them were at that moment in the school's library: Mr. Northington, the assistant principal, and Rebecca Dewey, the school librarian.

"That is not her name!" says the girl. "That's the system they use in the library for organizing the books!"

"Well, it is a name as well. It is the name of the man who invented that system, and Miss Dewey happens to be related to him. That's why she went into library work in the first place."

"Oh. I guess that makes sense. But what were they doing in the library at night?"

"I'm sure Miss Dewey had more work most days than she could ever hope to finish," says the mother. "But in Mr. Northington's case, there was more to it than that."

In addition to being the school librarian, Miss Dewey was also (and more importantly) the object of Mr. Northington's affection. Once he noticed that she had decided to stay late at the school, he did the same, pretending to be extremely busy. He stopped by the library and asked very politely if he could take Miss Dewey out to dinner.

"Oh, Edward," she said. "That's sweet of you, and I am a bit hungry."

Her smile and the sudden use of his first name left Mr. Northington feeling slightly dazed.

"It's such a shame I have all this work to do this evening," she continued, pointing to the box of books she was unpacking.

"Well," said Mr. Northington, in his most authoritative voice, "I think it would be perfectly fine if you left the rest of that until tomorrow. As the principal, I—"

"Assistant principal," she gently corrected him.

"I would be glad to get some of the children to help you after school. In fact, I insist on it."

"That's kind," she said. "But I think it's best if I do it myself."

"Didn't she like him?" asks the girl.

"I think she did like him. Perhaps she just didn't realize it yet. And anyway, she didn't want to deal with all the gossip and the teasing from the children."

"I can understand that," says the girl. "Northington and Dewey sitting in a tree . . ."

"My point exactly."

Mr. Northington returned to his office, not yet completely prepared to give up for the night. "She did say she was hungry," he was thinking. Then he had an idea. If Miss Dewey would not go out to dinner with him, he would bring dinner to her. Rushing around the corner to a small gourmet cheese shop, he forced himself inside the door just as the proprietor was pulling down the front shade.

"We're closing," the man said.

"This is an emergency!" Mr. Northington cried.

"A *cheese* emergency?"

"A love emergency."

"Oh, Mother," groans the girl.

"Just listen," the mother insists.

Luckily for Mr. Northington, the shop owner was a bit of a romantic. He packed up a lovely picnic supper inside a large wicker basket and even tossed in some gold candlesticks (from the shop's front window), which Mr. Northington promised to return the next day. Northington took these treasures to the school. When he got back to the library, Miss Dewey was nowhere to be seen. Northington sighed and prepared to admit defeat. Then he saw a small slice of light coming from beneath her office door at the rear of the library. So, quickly and quietly he arranged his feast on one of the library tables.

Then he tapped on Miss Dewey's door and said, "I'm sorry to disturb you, but I've brought you a food, some food, a . . ."

Mr. Northington got tongue-tied around Miss Dewey quite often. He led her out of the office and gestured toward the food with a flourish.

"Shall we?" he asked.

Clearly, he had hoped to impress her with this spontaneous and gallant gesture.

So imagine his surprise when instead of swooning with joy, Miss Dewey began to inspect the food and said, "Pack that up at once!"

"But why?"

"Why? I don't allow anyone to *eat* in the library. And just look at what you've brought here: a sharp knife and tree nuts? In a school? Are you mad?"

"She does have a point," says the girl. "A lot of people are allergic."

"Miss Dewey was a very sensible young lady. You could have learned a lot from her."

"I'm sorry!" Mr. Northington cried. "Of course, you're right. As usual."

And though these words would seem to be music to any woman's ears, it took a bit to calm Miss Dewey down.

"It's—it's just . . . ," he stammered. "How else am I to get your attention? You don't notice me at all. You spend all your time talking to the children."

"Oh, Edward," said Miss Dewey.

"Mother!" exclaims the girl. "I thought you promised she was sensible."

"She didn't say it the way you think."

"Edward," she said, "is this your idea of how to attract a woman? By bringing her a hunk of cheese?"

"No," he mumbled, hanging his head.

"I'm a librarian, not a mouse," said Miss Dewey, maneuvering Mr. Northington toward the door.

"Will I see you tomorrow?" he asked hopefully.

"Mr. Northington," she reminded him. "You'll see me every day. I work here."

## MISSING ARABELLA

For once, Henrietta was the only one who would sleep well. While her sister walked through the damp darkness of her first night on the road, Henrietta watched the rain slide down her bedroom window on Chillington Lane. She had gotten used to the strange room at Aunt Priscilla's. The cats, while not overly friendly, had stopped hissing and learned to tolerate their new companion, as cats will. And Henrietta, for her part, was trying her best to fit in at her strange new household.

She had spent the afternoon raking leaves in Aunt Priscilla's unruly back garden, scooping them into large piles that stood between the broken trellises and crumbling wooden archways. Priscilla's garden was nothing like the one at home, yet it still called to mind games of hide-and-seek with Arabella. Henrietta was lost in thought, remembering her sister, when Priscilla's voice startled her.

"Someone is here to see you," Priscilla announced from the back door.

And for one hopeful moment, Henrietta believed that her sister might step through the back door to join her in the ruined garden, that fond memories alone might be enough to make her materialize. Instead, Inez was there, holding a book under her arm.

"I think you need a warmer jacket," she said, by way of greeting. "Your cheeks are bright pink."

"I love it out here," Henrietta said. "I guess I miss my mother's garden."

"Well," said Inez, "when you're ready to come in and warm up, have a look at this."

And she handed her a new book. Henrietta opened it and sniffed the pages.

"New-book smell," Henrietta replied. "Almost as good as burning leaves."

"Burning leaves?" asks the girl by the fire. "Isn't that illegal?"

"Not in the old days," says the mother.

"That makes air pollution!" insists the girl.

"It probably does," says the mother. "But it smells wonderful."

"You'll like it even more when you have a chance to read it," Inez said fondly.

And they went inside to share some tea and some butter cookies Inez had brought in a small bakery box tied with string.

"You should offer your friend some soup," suggested Aunt Priscilla. "Your last batch wasn't half-bad."

"Is that a compliment?" asks the girl.

"Coming from Aunt Priscilla, it was high praise indeed," says the mother.

Then Priscilla excused herself for a nap and left Inez and Henrietta to their plate of cookies. (Neither one of them really wanted the soup.)

Henrietta was grateful for the snack. Though she tried to be a good sport, the food at Aunt Priscilla's was difficult to adjust to. She managed most nights to get away without consuming much by hiding the solid bits in her napkin and slipping some to the cats. The rest she swallowed as fast as she could, hoping to taste it as little as possible. The obvious downside was that Henrietta was often hungry.

Since she was now the chief cook and bottle washer at Aunt Priscilla's...

"The chief cook?" asks the girl.

"Just an expression," says the mother. "They were quite alone. Apart from the cats."

"And Inez," says the girl.

"Yes. Just this once, Inez. But she could stay for only a short time before she had to leave to reopen the shop."

Delicious as the butter cookies were, they weren't enough to fill Henrietta's stomach for a full day, and neither was the odd, thin stew they had for dinner. So later that evening, as Henrietta stood at the window watching the rain, she felt her stomach rumble. And she decided to slip down to the kitchen, where she began to rummage around, looking for anything she might be willing to eat. The grocery box that had been delivered to their door that day contained merely the usual, horrible ingredients for Aunt Priscilla's bizarre recipes. Snacks were hard to come by.

The kitchen was huge. Dried herbs hung from a pot rack, and there were many tall cabinets, but Henrietta never had much of a chance to investigate them; her time in the kitchen was always occupied by cooking or washing the seemingly endless stacks of dishes that formed by the sink.

This particular night, however, as her sister was looking for a place to rest and her parents were busy worrying about where Arabella was, Henrietta was enjoying a moment's peace.

"You're always saying you need one of those," says the girl.

"All mothers do."

Henrietta got hers because Aunt Priscilla fell asleep in front of the fire. And Henrietta climbed on a stool and opened a tall, creaky cabinet in the kitchen. There, beneath a soft film of dust, she found a small collection of spices, including her personal favorite: cinnamon. Henrietta grabbed the jar and was about to go to work when she glanced out the kitchen window and saw that the rain had started to turn to snow—the first, light, magical snowfall of the year was drifting down from the sky, outlining each branch in Priscilla's neglected garden. Without stopping for a coat, Henrietta went through the back door, tilted her head to the sky, and began to catch snowflakes on her tongue. She thought of all the times she and Arabella had made snow angels together, spreading their arms wide in the glistening white.

"Aunt Priscilla shouldn't miss this," she thought.

And she ran to wake Priscilla, rushing to her chair by the fire, and stopping only at the last moment when doubt overtook her. Priscilla must have sensed her presence, for she opened her eyes and said, "You're all wet!"

"It's snowing," Henrietta said. "Come and see."

And she grabbed Priscilla's gnarled hand and helped her out of the chair. Perhaps she was still half-asleep; perhaps she was just too startled to resist. But moments later Priscilla was standing at the threshold looking out at the snow. Because she paused there, Henrietta had to take her by both hands and tug. The momentum sent them spinning in a circle, arms locked, as snowflakes fell on their hair and eyelashes. The sound that came next was more like a small dog barking than anything human, and Henrietta would have been hard-pressed to identify it in any case because (she suddenly realized) she had never heard Priscilla laugh.

When she had finished, the world seemed still and silent in the way it only can during a snowfall. Priscilla drew a long breath and sighed.

"We should go in," she said.

"But it's so lovely," Henrietta protested.

Aunt Priscilla looked toward the house. When she turned her gaze back toward her niece, Henrietta could see that her expression had shifted. Aunt Priscilla looked uncomfortable.

"She's probably cold," suggests the girl.

"I think she felt nervous," explains the mother. "About being outside."

And just like that, the spell was broken. Priscilla returned to doze by the fire, and Henrietta went back to the kitchen alone to reclaim the little jar of cinnamon she had abandoned on the counter.

Every few minutes she would tiptoe back to see that Priscilla was still asleep. Finally she stepped too close in her inspection, and Priscilla's eyelids fluttered, then snapped open.

"What?" she asked.

"It's just me again," Henrietta told her, stepping back. "I didn't mean to startle you."

"Have you finished your chores?"

"Almost," Henrietta said.

"Then off to bed with you," Aunt Priscilla said.

Henrietta sighed.

"What's the matter now?" Priscilla demanded.

"Even if I go to bed," Henrietta said sadly, "I won't be able to sleep."

"Child, are you implying the room isn't what it ought to be?"

"No," said Henrietta with a catch in her voice. "I just don't like sleeping alone."

And as she stood there trying to explain it all to Aunt Priscilla, Henrietta remembered countless whispered conversations in the dark with her sister and the way they had to stifle their laughter sometimes so the grown-ups wouldn't hear. She remembered winter nights in flannel nightgowns and white kneesocks when they would tent their blankets and kick against them and watch the bright sparks of static electricity flash like indoor stars.

"You'll be asleep," Priscilla insisted. "It won't matter."

"I know," Henrietta said, a tear sliding down her cheek. "I guess I'm just missing Arabella."

"Oh," said Aunt Priscilla. And she patted Henrietta's hand with her stiff, bony fingers.

"Aunt Priscilla?" Henrietta asked, sniffing. "Would you like a bedtime snack?"

"Don't believe in them," Priscilla said firmly.

"Why don't you try it?" Henrietta asked.

"I suppose it can't hurt," Priscilla said. "Just this once."

So Henrietta returned to the kitchen to collect the cinnamon toast and brought it out to Aunt Priscilla by the fire. And they both fell asleep still tasting the gritty sweetness, happily unaware that it would be their last full night together in that house.

## ARABELLA HAS A BIT OF A FRIGHT

As melancholy as it was to walk past the well-lit houses of the town, returning to the empty countryside was even worse. Without the streetlights to guide her, Arabella had no idea whether she was still on course. It wasn't her original idea or first choice to spend the night in the woods. That's simply where she found herself when she finally and for good ran out of energy.

The woods that night were terrifying and lovely all at once. The dark center of her new world. The rain had stopped, but the canopy of trees above her still dripped, and Arabella touched the wet leaves with her fingertips. Her thoughts kept turning to Henrietta, to the fateful day when Henrietta had been sent away, and she—despite her favored status—had done nothing to intervene.

Arabella wished now that she had set out to save her sister sooner—that she had defended her with words from the start. Then this whole lonely journey would not have been needed. But there was no going back. There was no going anywhere—tired as she was. She sank down onto the cool, wet earth beneath a tree and began to cry.

The moon above was clear and full; she could see its rippled reflection in the surface of the stream she had crossed. The wind blew. And in the distance she heard dogs barking and the muffled cries of people moving through the woods.

Were they coming for her? Were they there to bring her home?

Arabella shivered and touched the silver whistle around her neck. If she used it, they might find her. And she could be home, safe in her warm bed. Maybe that was what she should do. Maybe it had all been a mistake thinking that she could find her way to Henrietta all alone.

Arabella pressed the whistle to her lips, and the moon hung in the dark sky as she considered the possibilities. A tear traced its way along her cheek, and she let the voices fade away.

Henrietta needed her. Henrietta needed her, so Arabella would go to her.

Arabella settled herself at the base of a tree and pretended to be calm, until finally she really was calm enough to close her eyes and go to sleep.

The wind blew, and leaves skittered across the ground. But Arabella slept on—oblivious to all of it. Her head tipped against her shoulder, and her gold hair curtained her beautiful face. Until a loud, eerie call awakened her.

"Whoo, whoo!"

She jumped to her feet, trying to remember where she was.

"Whoo, whoo!" came the cry again.

Now she was wide awake, and it took only a moment for Arabella to spot the owl's yellow eyes in the dark. Its head swiveled toward her with alarming speed. Arabella yelped and crouched down low to watch the owl. She clutched the silver whistle Gus had given her. As her hand closed around it, the owl took flight—a flurry of wings

in the darkness. Then all around her was quiet again. Too quiet. So quiet that she could hear everything: small birds trilling and branches snapping. Earlier she had been afraid of being alone in the woods. Now Arabella realized that she was only one among many. There were creatures all around her. She even thought she saw a firefly in the distance, though she knew those were long gone, like the warm air of summer.

"I don't like it," says the girl.

"What?"

"Her being out there all alone. I wish the silver whistle were magic."

"Well," says the mother, "having it did make her feel more sure of herself—even though she didn't use it. And whatever makes you feel safe, whatever gives you confidence, there's a kind of magic in that."

In fact, Arabella was now as curious as she was frightened. She watched the little light in the distance and realized that it didn't wink on and off as a firefly would, but held steady, like a night-light. She tiptoed toward it, through the damp leaves and fallen twigs. It seemed a great distance away because she was moving so slowly. With each step, she could feel her

heart beating against her chest. It was a candle she saw—
a candle planted in white sand inside a glass canning jar.

"Where have I seen that jar before?" Arabella wondered.

Shadows were everywhere, and she thought she heard
something large and alive moving toward her. Arabella took
a deep breath.

"She screamed!" shouts the girl.

"No," says the mother.

She smiled and ran forward. She threw her arms around
him and said his name.

"Gus."

## TOGETHER—ALL ALONE

"You followed me," Arabella said softly.

"I couldn't help it," Gus replied. "It was so brave of you to set out on your own."

Arabella looked around at the dark woods, at the small candle Gus had lit. It all seemed so much more manageable now that he was here.

"Thank you," she told him, feeling suddenly shy with gratitude.

And they nestled in together beneath the falling leaves. Gus gave her his jacket, which was huge and warm.

"You'll be too cold to sleep now," she protested.

"No," he said. "I can't sleep anyway."

"Then I'll keep you company."

They rested there in the glow of the candle, and the noises all around them seemed softer now—less frightening. Time eased by, and the silence between them was the comfortable kind between friends.

"Are you awake?" she couldn't help asking.

"Entirely."

"Do you think I'll find her, Gus? Or should I just go home?"

"You have to find her. Anyway, she's not very far away. She never was. It just seems that way because you've never been on your own before."

"Have you?" she asked.

"Of course not," said Gus. "I'm only eleven."

Arabella reached out to touch his hand. "I keep forgetting," she said. "Sorry."

"It's okay," he assured her. "Sometimes I wish I were on my own."

Arabella wondered if he was thinking of his parents. She remembered their loud fight as she said goodbye to Gus.

"My family's not perfect either," she told him. "They never should have sent her away. My sister. And it's really all my fault too."

Though Gus couldn't see it, Arabella's face had clouded over.

"Don't be too hard on yourself," Gus said. "It's difficult to refuse when everyone lets you have your way. People do the same thing to me."

"I suppose," Arabella said.

"Everyone forgets to be fair sometimes," Gus said.

"Mother," says the girl. "Do you think Arabella's mean?"

"No," says the mother with a smile. "I think Arabella is changing."

Arabella grew quiet, thinking. At last, she slept, sure that when morning came, they would find their way to the road, the road that would eventually lead to Henrietta.

##  ESCAPE

With Gus by her side, Arabella felt entirely safe. Yet Gus was not the only one who was following Arabella on her journey. The police had set out hours earlier with dogs and flashlights and more volunteers than they really wanted. Finding nothing as the night wore on, the civilians turned back and went home to sleep in their warm beds, their fatigue winning out in the end, despite their best intentions. Only the chief and a few of his senior officers remained; they were determined to press a bit farther into the woods before giving up for the night. And Gus, a light sleeper under the best of circumstances, woke to the sound of their approach.

"Arabella!" he whispered, nudging her awake. "Get up! Someone's coming."

The rustling was louder now. They heard one of the dogs bark.

"Hurry," Gus urged. "We can't waste any time. We have to get across the stream."

"The stream?" Arabella asked.

"It's the best way to lose the dogs," Gus said.

He grabbed her hand; she grabbed her bookbag. They were off.

"How deep is it?" Arabella asked as they reached the edge of the stream.

Gus had already waded in, and he turned back to face her. "What?"

"Gus," she said, her voice trembling just slightly. "Have I mentioned that I don't know how to swim?"

"Here," he said, crouching at her feet. "Get up on my shoulders."

Now, the truth was that Arabella was also a bit afraid of heights, but this didn't seem the best time to mention it.

"Hang on!" Gus ordered as he plunged back into the water and began to walk downstream.

The sky had clouded over, and a light snow started to fall. They could still hear the dogs barking in the distance when they climbed out onto the bank, damp and missing one shoe (Arabella's). But gradually the sound faded, the flashlight beams swung away from them, and Arabella's pounding heart began to slow.

"Gus," Arabella whispered. "Do you think they're gone?"

"Absolutely," Gus assured her. "It's just us."

And so it was—just the two of them in the quiet, snowy woods.

### ❧ MR. NORTHINGTON ON THE CASE ❧

That next morning, as Arabella and Gus were dusting themselves off in the chilly woods, Mr. Northington arrived at the school bright and early as usual. His failed attempt at a picnic dinner had left him feeling far too embarrassed to stop by the library for his customary chat with Miss Dewey. Instead, he went straight to Principal Rothbottom's office, where he learned all about the missing Osgood girl.

"Have they found her?" Northington asked.

"Not yet," said Principal Rothbottom wearily. "They searched last night with no luck. Anyway, they aren't even sure what has happened. She may have been kidnapped for all we know, though there's been no note."

"Kidnapped?" Northington asked. "Does the family have that kind of money?"

"I suppose they do," said Principal Rothbottom impatiently. "But that's hardly the point. The girl's safety is the issue."

"Of course," said Northington, beginning to daydream.

"Northington!" yelled Principal Rothbottom. "Are you listening to me? I'll need you to interview the children. Find out if any of them know anything."

. . .

So Northington spent the morning asking the children if they had any idea where Arabella might be. Of course, most of them were genuinely unaware of her whereabouts, and they were able to tell the truth quite easily. But then there were the children in Arabella's own class, and they knew full well what Arabella had done. They had helped her do it.

At recess, Brendan Crowhurst gathered everyone together on the playground for an emergency meeting.

"Listen," he said. "Nobody says a word about what really happened, or we're all in trouble!"

"*You* listen!" said Lacey. "The police were at my house yesterday asking all sorts of questions."

"The police!" Eliza Sneedle exclaimed.

But Brendan silenced her with a look.

"My dad was out last night with the search party, and he says they think she might be lost in the woods," said another boy. "They're going back today to keep looking."

"Let them!" yelled Brendan.

"You're too loud," said Lacey. "The teachers will hear."

"I say we didn't really have anything to do with this," Brendan said, puffing out his chest and daring them to disagree. "We didn't make her leave."

"We tricked Miss Brittlewhite," Eliza insisted.

"So?"

And nobody could really argue with that, as cruelty toward substitute teachers is a right of childhood.

"Really?" asks the girl.

"Of course not," says the mother. "But there's little that can stop it."

Eventually, of course, Brendan Crowhurst had his way, and everyone agreed that it was too late to tell the truth now. They would keep their secret and wait to see what happened.

"What did happen?" asks the girl.

"That's what I'm getting to," says the mother.

Later that morning, Principal Rothbottom announced that he planned to leave for an early lunch. He instructed Mr. Northington to call the Osgoods and update them on the school's investigation.

"I'll do better than that," said Mr. Northington. "I'll visit them myself."

"Good idea," said Principal Rothbottom, secretly hoping he would not come to regret it. "The personal touch."

"Close the door, will you?" Northington asked, smiling as the principal left. Then Northington pulled a sandwich out of his bottom drawer and nibbled on it as he reviewed the list of students he had yet to interview. An hour later, as he was leaving to visit the Osgoods, Northington brushed past a tearful Miss Dewey outside the teachers' lounge, where Arabella was now the only topic of conversation.

"It's awful, Mr. Northington, isn't it?" Miss Dewey asked. "That poor girl."

"You're not to worry, Miss Dewey," he said, squaring his shoulders. "I'm certain we'll find her. I give you my word."

"Thank you," she said, squeezing his hand. "I know we can count on you. Well, I must get back."

Mr. Northington stared at her. She was even more beautiful with her deep brown eyes swimming with tears. Mr. Northington continued to stare while Miss Dewey looked from his face to her own hand, which was still caught in his.

"Oh!" he said, startled. And he dropped her hand quickly. "Yes. Yes, of course."

Then Northington hurried away—remembering, after a few moments, that he was headed to the Osgoods.

"Do you think he can really find her?" asks the girl.

"Well, he has a powerful motive to try," says the mother.

"Miss Dewey?"

"Exactly."

## ❧ THE MISSING POSTER ☙

When Northington arrived at the house, the living room was crowded; he entered quietly when Rose let him in, and he took in the scene. Mrs. Osgood was wringing her hands and asking "What will we do?" over and over again. Rose offered tea to everyone while Mr. Osgood—looking completely exhausted—consulted with the police.

"We found no trace of her in the woods last night," the chief of police was saying. "And usually at this juncture we would be receiving a note from the kidnappers threatening to kill the, ah, the victim, kidnappee—"

"Kill?" shrieked Mrs. Osgood.

"It's just what they say, ma'am. You know, if you don't send the money, blah, blah, blah . . ."

"What?"

"You'll find her body, blah, blah, blah . . ."

"Please!" yelled Mr. Osgood. "You are frightening my wife."

Standing in the corner, Mr. Northington admired Mr. Osgood and thought how wonderful it would be to protect Miss Dewey so gallantly.

"My point, Mrs. Osgood," said the chief of police, "is that we have no ransom note. Therefore I have to conclude that your daughter wasn't kidnapped for ransom at all. So there's nothing to be upset about!"

He smiled.

"Oh," said Mrs. Osgood in a small voice.

Mr. Osgood sighed. "I am delighted to hear she hasn't been kidnapped. But as you can see, she isn't here either! We still have a rather large problem."

"Yes?" asked the chief.

"Where *is* she?" asked Mr. Osgood, exasperated.

The chief shrugged. "Ran away? Drowned in the river?"

"Oh no!" yelled Mrs. Osgood. "Oh dear, oh dear, oh dear!"

"Perhaps I can help," said Mr. Northington, stepping forward.

"Who are you?" asked the Osgoods.

Mr. Northington introduced himself, with handshakes all around, and explained that he was conducting a thorough investigation (he loved those words) into Arabella's disappearance on the school's behalf.

"As well you might be!" snapped Mrs. Osgood. "Since you were the ones who lost my girl in the first place."

"We don't know that, dear," said Mr. Osgood.

"But we are prepared to find her," said Mr. Northington. "And I, for one, think the first step should be . . ." He paused and looked desperately toward the chief of police.

"A missing poster!" the chief of police shouted. "Send for the sketch artist!"

"Nonsense," said Mrs. Osgood. "I'm an artist myself. And nobody knows a child better than her own mother."

She sniffed and sent Rose running for her art supplies.

"Yes," said Mr. Osgood. "We can do the poster. Leave it to us."

As Mrs. Osgood was busy sketching, the chief said, "I think we should offer a reward."

"The school would be glad to assist," Mr. Northington said. "Perhaps a carnival, to raise money."

"That's ridiculous," said Mr. Osgood. "We haven't got that kind of time."

"A penny drive?"

"A penny drive! How will that help?" Mr. Osgood yelled. "We need to offer a substantial and immediate reward."

"He's right," the girl says.

"Well, pennies do add up, as I keep trying to tell you," the mother says. "But, of course, pennies weren't enough, and what the Osgoods had themselves wasn't enough, and eventually they decided to turn to the only person they could think of who might be able to help. Can you guess who it was?"

"Miss Brittlewhite."

"No. Of course not. Teachers never have any money."

"The police?"

"They were doing all they could. No, the Osgoods decided that as difficult as it would be, they would need to speak to Aunt Priscilla about donating the reward money."

"She's got to help us," Mrs. Osgood said.

"My dear, she may not have that kind of money at hand."

"Nonsense!" Mrs. Osgood shouted. "Let her sell that giant emerald ring she wears or offer it as a reward."

"Emerald?" asked Mr. Northington.

"Wait," says the girl. "Aunt Priscilla is rich?"

"Quite."

"But she lives in such squalor!"

"Nice word," says the mother.

"How's the sketch coming?" asked the chief of police.

"Nearly finished," said Mrs. Osgood, a note of pride in her voice.

"And I've typed the message to paste beneath it!" said Mr. Osgood, rushing in from his study.

"What's this supposed to be?" asked the chief, staring at the drawing.

"Why, it's Arabella! And quite a good likeness, if I do say so myself."

"Why are her ears on top of her head?"

"Those aren't her ears, you fool. That's a bow in her hair. Anyone can see that."

The chief sighed and reached for the note Mr. Osgood was handing him.

"What's that supposed to say?" he asked, looking down at the note.

*,oddo,mh hot;/ Stsnr;;s Pdhppf/ Trestf pggrtrf.*

"Oh, doe, hot stersen, trest oh gert? Ogre? Hot star? Ogre person?"

"This isn't charades!" yelled Mr. Osgood. "Clearly it says: 'Missing girl. Arabella Osgood. Reward offered.'"

"You moved your hands again!" Mrs. Osgood yelled at her husband. "You're a terrible typist. Where are your spectacles?"

"I think we'll take it from here," said the chief of police.

## ❧ THE UNEXPECTED VISITORS ❧

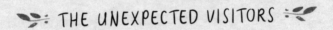

Aunt Priscilla, you see, had piled up quite a fortune during her days as a famous actress, though you would never know it to look at her house. And she certainly wasn't spending it on gourmet meals. In fact, she wasn't spending much of it at all. Still, the Osgoods knew it would be hard to get her to part with any of it even in such extreme circumstances as these. But they had to go to Aunt Priscilla in person and make their case. And they had to do it right away because, though none of them had given a moment's thought to visiting Henrietta, they were desperate to do all they could for Arabella. So they piled into the Osgoods' car: Mr. Osgood,

Mrs. Osgood, Rose, Principal Rothbottom (who had joined the group after lunch), Mr. Northington, the chief of police, and Mrs. Osgood's lapdog, Muffin.

"Isn't that too many people for one car?" asks the girl.

"Yes. They decided it was. They asked Mr. Northington to get out."

"How rude!" says the girl.

"Well," says the mother, "the car was becoming noisy. Muffin was barking, and Mrs. Osgood, in her satin robe, was sniffling loudly."

"She still isn't dressed?"

"They tried to make her, but she refused, and they were in a hurry, so they just threw a blanket round her shoulders. I used to do it with you all the time when you were younger."

They left Mr. Northington behind and resettled themselves for the trip. As soon as they started off, Mr. Osgood was discussing strategy with the chief of police, Principal Rothbottom was saying over and over again how terribly sorry he was that this whole thing had happened in the first place, and Muffin, of course, was still barking loudly and nipping at the chief of police's ankles. They went along that

way down a half dozen country roads, disturbing the residents of the nearby small towns, including Gus's parents, who had just taken up their loud fight right where they had left off yesterday and were too engrossed in it to notice that Gus was missing.

At last they came to Aunt Priscilla's house. They pulled into the driveway in a huge rush, barking and weeping and tooting the horn. Henrietta heard the noise from the kitchen and ran to the front window just in time to see her father's car pull into the driveway. So many people tumbled out of it that she had a hard time identifying everyone at first. Some of the voices were familiar, of course, and in the mix she heard the voices of both her parents. A huge rush of relief and joy filled her heart because she imagined that they had come to retrieve her.

"That's too sad," says the girl. "She's getting her hopes up for nothing."

"Don't be such a pessimist," says the mother.

Henrietta watched as the group made their way to the door, but she didn't dare answer it once she caught sight of the police. And, after all, it was still Aunt Priscilla's house. Henrietta ran instead toward her room, stopping at the top of the stairs when curiosity got the better of her. Priscilla, for her part, was leisurely petting a cat (the one they now called Professor Wiggles) and considering making a late lunch of the cold fish soup they had eaten the night before for dinner.

"Not the soup again! And cold! That's even more disgusting."

"No. I think it was actually a bit better cold."

"Cold soup?"

"Listen, there are lots of cold soups. Gazpacho, vichyssoise . . ."

"Mother!"

"Well, it really doesn't matter anyway because when Priscilla heard the racket outside, she forgot all about the soup and rushed to the door. She wasn't keen about the outside world even when it kept to itself, so you can imagine how she felt about it knocking on her door uninvited."

"But they're her family."

"True enough, but she wasn't the sort of person with a lot of family feeling."

Aunt Priscilla went to the door and put her eye to the peephole, but she couldn't see a thing. Unfortunately, Mr. Osgood was doing the same thing on his side of the door, and they really weren't getting anywhere. Mrs. Osgood was taking matters into her own hands and had started to push through the dense bushes in front of the house in order to peek in the front windows. And they might have stood there all day if the chief of police hadn't fought his way to the front and started banging on the door with his nightstick.

"Open up!" the chief of police commanded.

From her side of the door, Aunt Priscilla took a step back and demanded to know who it was.

"It's Osgood, Aunt Priscilla," yelled Mr. Osgood.

"Osgood, you can't speak to me that way!"

"That wasn't me, Aunt Priscilla. That was the chief of police."

"Police?"

"Don't panic her," advised the nanny.

"I'll explain everything," Mr. Osgood promised, "if you'll just open the door. Please. It's a dire emergency."

"He doesn't really have to say that, does he? Dire and emergency. If it's—"

"Some people are prone to exaggeration, I suppose," says the mother.

"Like Mr. Northington and the cheese emergency?"

"Indeed."

Eventually, Aunt Priscilla unbarred the door. It took some doing because she had an amazing number of locks on it. It was more like a safe at the bank than a front door, really.

The chief of police was most impressed. "She certainly has gone to pains to secure the perimeter."

## AUNT PRISCILLA TO THE RESCUE?

At last they were all inside Aunt Priscilla's front parlor, which was dusty and dark, even during the day. There had never been this many people inside Priscilla Renfrew's house at one time, and the cats were completely discombobulated by the commotion. They gave out little yowls and scurried for the corners of the rooms, where they crouched behind plant stands and coat racks and hissed loudly. Aunt Priscilla, being quite unused to company, wasn't sure how to act. She didn't do the usual things, like offering them a seat or putting on a kettle so that they all might have some tea. They had to take matters into their own hands, and they did. Principal Rothbottom took off his jacket, cleared some space on the crowded furniture, and asked Priscilla if he might open the drapes. She frowned, then sighed heavily.

"If you must," Priscilla said.

"That's rude!" says the girl.

"Well, consider the source," says her mother.

And Rose, the nanny, said, "We're all a bit chilly. Do you suppose we might have a cup of tea? I'd be glad to assist if you'd show me. . . ."

Aunt Priscilla just pointed one bony, bejeweled finger toward the kitchen door.

Mrs. Osgood, who was not about to help in any way, just drew her blanket around her shivering shoulders and looked aggrieved.

"Aggrieved?"

"Let's see," says the mother. "It's sort of a cross between sad and put out."

"Oh," says the girl.

Mr. Osgood rushed to find his wife a place on the sofa. "Sit down, my dear," he said.

She did, and a cloud of ancient dust puffed up all around her, causing a fit of coughing. They had to call out to Rose in the kitchen to bring some water.

The chief of police, who was pacing in front of the fire, was eager to get things started. "We're here," he said, "on a matter of urgent business."

Now this was very confusing to Henrietta, who was still hiding at the top of the stairs. Henrietta believed that her parents had come to take her home and would at any moment ask to see her or even, overtaken by grief and regret, come rushing up the stairs to find her. But that didn't seem to be what was happening. She stood at the top of the steps—leaning forward to be sure to hear every word—and these last words about urgent business were most alarming. Suddenly she was afraid that she was in trouble of some sort, but what sort of trouble could be bad enough to bring the police? True, she had entertained some very nasty fantasies about Aunt Priscilla since she came, but they couldn't put you in jail just for those, could they?

Downstairs, the chief of police was saying, "Miss Renfrew, I'll come straight to the point. A situation has developed, an emergency, really. And though we hate to bother you with it, as it really isn't any of your affair, nevertheless, we feel, after careful consideration of all the facts and pondering the possible outcomes and examining every prudent contingency, it is our considered opinion that—"

"Oh, for pity's sake!" yelled Mr. Osgood. "Come to the point."

"She's missing!" sobbed Mrs. Osgood. "Our girl is gone!"

"Nonsense," said Aunt Priscilla. "She's around here somewhere. Out in the kitchen probably."

"*No!*" yelled the Osgoods.

"I should think so. I sent her there myself to make the soup and feed the bat."

"Oh, not *that* girl," said Mrs. Osgood. "Not Henrietta! We're talking about Arabella!"

Well, at the top of the stairs, Henrietta was a mass of conflicted emotion. She was surprised and alarmed, most of all, to hear that her twin was missing. She felt a small thrill, after such a long time, to hear her own name on her mother's lips, even in passing. And mixed with it all was the familiar disappointment that this current conversation, this urgent visit, this huge fuss, like everything else in her life, was not about her but about the only one who really mattered: her sister, Arabella.

"You've simply got to help us," Mrs. Osgood was saying now, sniffling into a handkerchief.

"We wouldn't have come," Mr. Osgood added, "if there were any other way."

"Well, I fail to see how I can be of any help," said Priscilla. "Clearly it's a matter for the police, and you seem to have brought the police here with you. Perhaps if they went out and started looking for the girl instead of pounding down my front door and bursting into my house uninvited, we might get somewhere."

"We've done our best, ma'am," said the chief of police. "We've tried to find her. But the longer she's gone the less likely that is."

"What?" yelled Mr. Osgood.

"Statistically speaking."

"But Arabella is not a statistic," says the girl.

"Of course not," says the mother. "That's why everyone is trying very hard to help her."

"The point is," said Mr. Osgood, "the police feel we need to offer a reward. A rather considerable sum."

"Then do it," snapped Priscilla.

"We haven't got it," admitted Mr. Osgood. "Not as much as we need."

"Go to the bank. Ask for a loan. Isn't that what people do when they run short? For pity's sake, you're a banker. Why would you come running to me for money?"

"Miss Renfrew," said Rose, drawing her aside and speaking softly, "the Osgoods, well, I'm sure they would find it terribly hard to say this to anyone, but they live a bit beyond their means, and so, you see, really, truly, just at the moment, they are a little low on cash. And we thought, naturally, since your great wealth and fame must have left you with quite a bit of savings, that you might, just this once of course, part with a little of it for the safety and welfare of your niece."

Well, Priscilla was quite torn at this point. On the one hand, she was flattered that the nanny had made reference to her being a wealthy and world-famous actress. On the other hand, Priscilla was quite protective of her store of riches. After all, she wasn't acting anymore, and whatever she had would have to last her for the rest of her life.

"We wouldn't ask," said Mrs. Osgood. "But I'm terrified she could be gone for good. She may be in serious danger."

"But she's not," says the girl.

"True. But mothers tend to picture the worst. Always remember that when it's time to call home."

Henrietta was a bit of a worrier as well, and this last proclamation was too much for her. Listening at the top of the stairs to the shocking news that she might never see Arabella again, Henrietta began to feel ill. First her head felt light; then she slumped against the wall and tumbled all the way down the stairs into the living room, landing on a few of the cats along the way and setting them howling.

## ❧ GUS IN DISGUISE ☙

Although her life was not really in imminent danger, Arabella did have troubles of her own. For one thing, she was missing a shoe. For another, she was cold, damp, and completely exhausted. But physical discomfort was really the least of her worries. No, what really troubled Arabella most was the thought that they were still being followed.

"Gus," she asked as they walked along, "do you think they'll come back? The men from last night?"

"The police?"

"The police! Is that who they were?"

"I imagine so. Who did you think they were?"

"I don't know. Robbers?"

Gus laughed. "Who would they be robbing in the middle of the woods? Bunnies and squirrels? No. They're searching for you."

"I thought they might be. But why the police?" Arabella asked. "I'm just trying to find my sister. I'm not a criminal."

"You disappeared. Your parents must be worried sick. They probably called the police right away."

Arabella stopped walking. She sat down on the ground and covered her face with her hands.

"Oh, Gus," she said, "I've made a mess of everything! All I wanted was a chance to see Henrietta again. And now I've upset everyone. And I don't even know if we're going the right way. I had a map, but it got all wet and smudgy."

She pulled it out of her pocket and thrust it toward Gus, who examined it for a moment.

"I think I can get us there," he said.

"Really?"

"Yes, but . . ."

"What?" she asked. "Tell me."

"Arabella, I can't promise that we won't get caught. We're out in broad daylight now. Someone may see us, you know."

"There must be something we can do," Arabella insisted. "Maybe we could disguise ourselves."

"Maybe," Gus said. "I have an idea."

"What's he going to do?" asks the girl.

"I can't tell you that," says the mother. "It'll spoil the surprise."

"You know I hate surprises," says the girl. "Out with it."

"Well, it just so happened the morning was a breezy one, and they were hoping to find some laundry hanging out that they might be able to borrow."

"Borrow? You mean steal, don't you?"

"No need to get hysterical," says the mother. "They didn't find any."

The day was too cold for hanging laundry on the line. They did, however, spot a wonderful porch with a number of coats and hats hanging on hooks near the door.

"We can't take those!" Arabella whispered to Gus. "Just give me your jacket again."

"It's too wet!"

"I'm not stealing," said Arabella.

"We need them!" Gus said. "You can bring them back later."

"Will they bring them back later?" asks the girl.

"Of course not," says the mother. "But at least they had good intentions."

While Gus hid behind the nearby fence, Arabella darted onto the porch and scooped up an armful of clothes.

"Here," she said, offering Gus a wide-brimmed straw hat with a pink flower.

"I can't wear this!" Gus said.

"Don't be so fussy. It's perfect. It will cover your face. Nobody will know it's you. Here, put this on too," she said, handing him a fuzzy pink cardigan.

"I'll look like my grandmother!" Gus said.

"I thought we agreed that we needed disguises."

"I never said you could dress me as a girl!" Gus said.

"Please!" Arabella said. "I'm in a lot of trouble, and you said you would help."

Gus glared at Arabella for a long moment before he slipped his arm into the pink sweater and pulled on the too-tight hat.

"At least it's warm," he muttered.

"You look very nice," Arabella told him, trying not to smile as she wrapped herself up in a large shawl.

## ❧ A CASE OF MISTAKEN IDENTITY ☙

Though Gus thought he knew where they were going, they didn't seem to be getting there very quickly. As the day wore on, Gus and Arabella continued trudging forward on weary limbs. And despite his naturally long stride, Gus was having as much trouble as Arabella, who had kicked off her remaining shoe and was now traveling in her stocking feet. In fact, Arabella noticed, Gus seemed to be limping.

"Are you all right?" she asked him.

"I'm fine," he said at first.

"Gus, you can hardly walk," Arabella said.

"It's my joints," he said. "Comes with the territory."

"The territory?"

Gus gestured from his waist toward his toes, pointing out the length of his leg.

"Oh," she said. "I'm sorry. I never realized. Let's rest."

And so they sat for a while.

"It's good of you to help me," Arabella said.

"Well, I know how much you must miss your sister. I'm sure your parents do too in their heart of hearts. Not to mention her friends."

"Oh, Henrietta doesn't have any friends. Just me."

"Oh," said Gus, and his face fell.

"She doesn't mind much," said Arabella. "I play with her when I have time."

"When you have time?" Gus asked.

"Well, all the time," Arabella said, though she felt as she said it that it wasn't completely true.

Gus pulled himself to his feet. "Let's get going."

"Wait, Gus, are you mad at me?"

He shook his head.

"Yes, you are," Arabella insisted. "You disapprove."

"Arabella," he said. "You are who you are. I can't expect you to understand how things are. For people like Henrietta. And me."

He mumbled the last two words, but, of course, his voice was still loud, and Arabella could hear him clearly.

"Then tell me," Arabella said.

"Tell you what?"

"What it's like to be you."

"Lonely," said Gus.

And the word sliced through the air and silenced her. And then they walked along for a long time without talking at all until they found themselves at the edge of a park, where Arabella saw a chance to rest. She took a seat on a park bench, and Gus sat down beside her. They scarcely moved for so long that they both fell sound asleep.

"Do you think that Gus is really mad at her?" asks the girl.

"Perhaps," says the mother. "But I suspect he'll get over it."

"Maybe he doesn't like her anymore," says the girl.

"I doubt that," says the mother. "Gus is a true friend, and true friendship is a sturdy thing."

When she awoke, Arabella felt much better—even though she was quite hungry. She and Gus grabbed some apples that had fallen from a nearby tree and ate them in huge, grateful bites, wiping the juice on their sleeves. It gave them enough energy to continue, which was fortunate because Arabella was much closer to her sister than she realized.

Walking down the next block, they came to a bookshop

and decided on impulse to stop there and ask for directions to Aunt Priscilla's house. Gus waited outside to keep watch and sent Arabella in on her own.

"Excuse me," Arabella said, smiling at the woman behind the counter.

"Why, Henrietta, I wasn't expecting you until next week," the woman said. "How lovely to see you, and in such fine spirits too! I don't think I've ever seen you smile like that."

"Henrietta!" said Arabella. "You know Henrietta?"

Now the shopkeeper was most confused. "You aren't . . . ," she said slowly.

"I'm her sister, her twin sister," Arabella explained.

"Oh my! Yes, of course. The one she sent the note to," said Inez.

"How do you know about the note?" Arabella asked.

"She was here when she wrote it," Inez said. "And I helped her mail it."

"Thank you!" Arabella said, throwing her arms around Inez.

Then Arabella stepped back and looked up at Inez, blushing with embarrassment for being so impulsive. "I know we just met, but maybe you could help me too. I want to go and see her, but I'm not sure I can find my aunt's house."

"Of course," said Inez. "Come with me."

Inez took Arabella into the back of the shop, where she drew a map of the town.

"It's quite a long walk," Inez said, glancing at Arabella's shoeless feet. "Why don't you rest a bit before you continue?"

"I have a friend waiting," said Arabella, gesturing toward the front of the shop.

Inez peeked out the front window. "So you do," she said, commenting not at all on Gus's size or his outfit. "Let's ask him in."

Arabella agreed. And the three of them sat in the back of the shop, snacking on cookies and studying the map Inez had drawn for them. They saw at once that they had taken an overly long and roundabout route to cover the distance they had traveled so far.

"Well," Inez said, "however far you've strayed off course, the main thing is that you've come all this way to visit. And Henrietta will be thrilled to see you."

It didn't seem accurate to call running away a visit. But it didn't seem prudent to correct her either. So Arabella just smiled again, and she and Gus thanked Inez for the food and the new map. Then they gathered their things and went out of the shop.

"We'll be there before you know it," Gus said.

Arabella smiled and nudged him. "Lead the way," she said.

## MORE BAD LUCK FOR HENRIETTA

Of course Henrietta had no idea that Arabella—far from being in any danger—was actually snacking on cookies with Inez. Henrietta had just been told that her sister was in grave danger. And after hearing this news, Henrietta, you will recall, collapsed in a heap at the bottom of the stairs, landing right in front of her nanny. Rose knelt down to examine her.

"Oh dear," said Rose. "She's fainted. We'd better get her some water."

"This is just like her," said Mrs. Osgood. "To be a bother at the worst possible moment when we're in the middle of something important. Just drag her over to the corner before someone trips on her while we sort this out."

"Yes," said Mr. Osgood. "We have no time to lose. Arabella may be in grave danger!"

"This is enough!" yelled Priscilla. "Clear out, all of you. Get out."

"You can't mean that," said Mrs. Osgood.

"But we've come to no conclusion," said Mr. Osgood.

"I think she wants us to go," said Rose.

"But you haven't asked her!" said Mrs. Osgood, elbowing her husband.

"I've asked her, my dear, and Aunt Priscilla has declined. She isn't going to supply the money."

"Not the money!" Mrs. Osgood yelled. "The ring!"

"The ring?" asked Aunt Priscilla.

"Yes!" said Mrs. Osgood. "The police think we should offer it as part of the reward."

Aunt Priscilla stood up and pointed at the chief of police, the emerald ring in question glinting on her finger. "If he thinks I'm giving up this ring, he is sadly mistaken!"

"She was the one who mentioned it first," said the chief of police, pointing at Mrs. Osgood.

"All they're doing is wasting time blaming each other," says the girl.

"Yes. They're being rather childish."

"That's not even a fair word, really. When you think about it," says the girl.

"Point taken," the mother replies.

Mrs. Osgood had started to cry again. She was beside herself at Aunt Priscilla's unwillingness to part with anything that might bring about Arabella's safe return.

"How can you be so selfish?" she demanded. "Have you no feelings at all?"

"You don't know what you're asking," Priscilla told her. "This ring is quite valuable. It's not some trinket."

"Valuable?" Mrs. Osgood said. "Valuable? What price would you set on Arabella's safe return?"

"Do you really think she isn't coming back?" asked a small voice from a corner of the room. And they all turned to see that Henrietta—while still very pale—had recovered enough to sit up and join the conversation. In fact, she stood up and walked on shaky legs toward Aunt Priscilla's chair. Henrietta picked up Aunt Priscilla's spotted, gnarled hand and studied the glittering emerald ring.

"I know it means a lot to you," she said. "Almost as much as my sister means to me."

The two locked eyes, and everyone in the room was absolutely quiet, waiting.

Finally Henrietta broke the silence. "Please?" she asked.

"Oh, all right!" said Priscilla, shrugging off Henrietta's immediate and urgent embraces.

"Thank you, Aunt Priscilla!" said Henrietta. "Thank you!"

The Osgoods were amazed at Priscilla's assent. They stood speechless for a moment, taking in the odd sight of their daughter Henrietta lifting and kissing Priscilla's gnarled hand.

"Here," said Priscilla at last, reaching to remove the emerald ring from her finger. She slid and twisted, but the ring would not clear her (rather large) knuckle.

"Let me help," said Mr. Osgood, grabbing her hand and pulling with all his might.

"Don't be so rough," said Henrietta.

"That's not going to work," said Mrs. Osgood. "Take her to the kitchen and use some soap."

They decided to try it, but they failed—miserably. Time was ticking by.

"We should cut it off," said the chief of police. "No time for half measures."

"Her finger?" says the girl.

"Of course not. That would be barbaric. No, he meant they could cut through the band to get the ring off."

"But that would ruin it," says the girl.

"That was the problem."

"Don't break it!" Mrs. Osgood was yelling.

By now the ring was wedged tightly on Priscilla's finger, and it wouldn't move in either direction.

"Her finger doesn't look right," said Rose. "I think we should take her to the doctor."

"Good thinking," said Principal Rothbottom.

"Maybe they can get it off," said the chief of police.

"I am *not* leaving this house!" said Aunt Priscilla.

"But she went out with Henrietta," says the girl.

"True," says the mother. "But until that night in the snow, Aunt Priscilla had not left that house in years. Going out was no small thing for her."

When Priscilla refused to leave the house, the room exploded in noise as everyone assembled began to yell at once about how urgently they needed her cooperation.

"My girl!" Mrs. Osgood yelled.

"It's getting late," the chief of police warned.

"Aunt Priscilla!" Mr. Osgood yelled.

Then, as they all fell silent for a moment, it was Henrietta who said the two words that finally moved Priscilla out of her chair.

Henrietta looked at Priscilla and said softly, "You promised."

"All right," Priscilla said, "let's go."

She wrapped herself in a dark cape . . .

"Like a witch," says the girl.

"She was terrified, really. Would a witch be terrified? She was pale and trembling when they got her into the car. She could hardly speak to tell them where to go. Sometimes she would just lift a finger and point."

"Couldn't Henrietta help?" asks the girl.

"She might have known the way," says the mother, "if they had remembered to invite her along."

The sad truth was that in their rush to help Arabella, they had forgotten all about Henrietta—as usual. So she was left behind and spent the evening as she always did—alone. Too tired to finish her chores and exhausted with worry, she passed out in front of the fire. In fact, she had pulled her chair a tad too close to the flames because a spark landed on the edge of her sweater, and she woke just in time to see it starting to burn. She jumped up, of course, screaming, and swatted at the flames with a newspaper.

"That's not what you do!" says the girl. "Stop, drop, and roll. Didn't they teach her anything in school?"

"Well, dear, she's missed quite a bit of school, and she's been spending her time cooking hideous food and reading fairy tales at the bookshop. You don't learn much that way."

But eventually Henrietta realized, even in her panic, that she could just slip out of her sweater, and she did. The bad part was that it really was burning now, not just the sweater but the chair and then the room. And so, not thinking clearly, Henrietta rushed back up the stairs toward her room.

"No!" yells the girl. "Now she's trapped."

"Exactly," says the mother.

## MR. NORTHINGTON JOINS THE SEARCH

While Henrietta was contemplating her doom, the adults in charge were busy with other things. The Osgoods, accompanied by the chief of police, the nanny, and the principal, were driving Aunt Priscilla to the hospital so her ring could be removed. And Mr. Northington, having been left behind at the start, had just completed a long day of interviewing students. He had twisted as many arms as he could, trying to learn the truth of Arabella's whereabouts.

"That's not allowed!" shouts the girl.

"Just an expression," the mother says. "No cause for alarm."

Now Northington was riding through the town, on the front half of his parents' old tandem bicycle, putting up the missing posters. As he rode, he pictured another sort of ride, one in which Miss Dewey was perched on the seat behind him, laughing at his jokes and whispering in his ear.

"That's not going to happen," says the girl.

"Love had made him optimistic," says the mother.

He thought of the missing girl as he rode. And he remembered Miss Dewey's tearful thanks to him for promising to rescue her. Suddenly Mr. Northington could see it all in his mind's eye: He would rescue the little girl, return her to her parents, collect the reward money (and the emerald ring Mrs. Osgood had mentioned). Then Miss Dewey would be his. How could she resist him? A hero who had rescued a little girl, a newly wealthy man with a beautiful ring to offer? The principal of her school.

"Assistant principal," says the girl. "And Miss Dewey isn't even his girlfriend yet."

"True. He was getting a bit ahead of himself."

But once he saw it all clearly, Northington knew that he was doing the wrong thing. Why should he hang these missing posters all over town so that anyone might find Arabella and earn the reward? True, the sketch didn't much resemble the girl (Mrs. Osgood wasn't much of an artist), but Mr. Northington didn't fancy any competition.

He retraced his steps and undid his work—pulling down the missing posters as fast as he could. As he was removing the last one, he saw one of the students he had interviewed earlier that day. A girl. What was her name? Elmira? Elvira?

"Eliza!" says the girl.

"Indeed."

"Oh no," says the girl.

"You there!" said Mr. Northington. "Come here a moment."

Eliza's mother had sent her to the store to buy some milk, and she was expecting her to return directly. Eliza was not to stop to speak to any strange men along the way. But, of course, she recognized Mr. Northington from school. If he had asked her to stop in the hallway of the school, she would have done so immediately. But outside the school, she hesitated.

"Little girl!" Mr. Northington said. "I'd like to speak to you."

Reluctantly, Eliza went over to him.

"We spoke earlier," Mr. Northington said. "About this Arabella Osgood business."

"Yes," said Eliza, remembering her promise to say nothing.

"You know the police are involved now, don't you?"

"I've heard that," Eliza said.

"And I bet a bright young lady like you might know something about it too," Northington said.

"I can't really talk now," Eliza told him. "I told my mother I'd hurry back."

"Oh, but this will only take a minute," Northington said. "Eliza, don't you think your mother would want you to do the right thing?"

Eliza looked down and studied her shoes, unsure of what to do.

"I think you know the answer," Northington cajoled.

Eliza, who prided herself on always knowing the answer, who spent the bulk of each school day with her hand stretched skyward in a constant, desperate bid to be called on, could take it no longer.

"She's on her way to her aunt's house!" Eliza yelled.

It was such a relief to say it finally that Eliza forgot for the moment all the promises they had made to Brendan Crowhurst.

"Her aunt?" Northington asked. "Priscilla? That's right! Priscilla . . ."

"Renfrew," said Eliza. "R as in 'rapid,' e, n, f, r, e, w. Renfrew."

"What?" asks the girl.

"Spelling bee champion," explains the mother.

"Good girl," said Mr. Northington as Eliza rushed away as fast as her legs would carry her.

## ❧ A MISHAP ☙

Northington was delighted by what Eliza Sneedle had divulged. He set out to find this Aunt Priscilla right away.

"Renfrew," he repeated aloud to himself as he rode.

"But he doesn't know where he's going!" says the girl.

"True," says the mother. "But sadly that wasn't enough to stop him."

"Renfrew," he said as he pedaled. "Ha, ha! Renfrew."

Mr. Northington was as excited as a child with a new toy. And his joy caused him to do something he definitely should not have done: he raised his hands off the handlebars.

He followed each twist and turn in the road, enjoying every bounce and bump, secure in the knowledge that he could locate Arabella and return as a hero who would win Miss Dewey's heart. And so, his mind was elsewhere and the sun was shining when he swerved off the road and crashed the bicycle into a large bush, jostling a low-hanging nest of wasps and unleashing their fury. Northington hopped off the tandem bike and began to run, still twisting and turning, with a cloud of angry wasps buzzing around his head.

"Was he stung?" asks the girl.

"Yes. Poor hapless fellow. He was," says the mother. "Repeatedly."

They chased and stung him until he fell to the ground.

"Was he still saying 'Renfrew'?"

"He was trying," says the mother.

"I shouldn't laugh," says the girl.

Northington's face and eyelids began to swell. His tongue puffed up in his mouth.

"Oh no," he tried to say. "Oh no," he tried again.

Northington wobbled away on his dented bicycle, which now swerved all of its own accord.

"I think I need a hothpital," he said to the first passerby he met.

## ❧ AT THE HOSPITAL ❧

And so it happened that Mr. Northington arrived at the hospital with his emergency just before the Osgoods got there with Aunt Priscilla and her swollen knuckle.

"Name?" asked the clerk at the admitting desk.

"Nothing-hon," he replied, his tongue now as thick as a sausage.

"Sir, everyone has a name," the clerk said sharply (she was used to dealing with the uncooperative and underinformed). "And I need yours."

"Nothing-hon," he repeated with great effort.

"My name, for example," said the clerk, "is Mrs. Sandsbury. Not hon. Not honey. Mrs. Sandsbury."

Mr. Northington, hugely frustrated by this point, stamped his foot like a balky horse.

"Perhaps you intend to spell it out," suggested Mrs. Sandsbury with a sigh.

Just then the front door opened and the Osgoods came through, trailing their nanny, Principal Rothbottom, the chief of police, Aunt Priscilla, and an overexcited, yipping Muffin.

"What's a yipping muffin?" asks the girl.

"Mrs. Osgood's little dog. Muffin."

"Oh," says the girl. "That wasn't what I was picturing. Now I feel silly."

Though Mr. Northington was having great difficulty identifying himself, Principal Rothbottom and Mrs. Osgood recognized him at once.

"There's that ridiculous fellow from the school," she said. "What's the matter with him?"

"It looks as though he's having some sort of a fit," Mr. Osgood suggested.

Muffin, drawn to the movement of Mr. Northington's stamping foot, clamped onto his ankle with her pointed little teeth.

Mrs. Sandsbury sighed heavily and called out for a wheelchair.

"Who is the owner of this dog?" Mrs. Sandsbury demanded.

"Mrs. Osgood," said the principal. "I believe that's your dog. Muffin."

Mrs. Osgood, who normally was quick to claim her prized pooch, looked around at the others as if expecting them to answer. "Dog?" her face seemed to say. "What dog?"

"We do not allow animals inside the hospital," said Mrs. Sandsbury as Muffin chased after the yowling Mr. Northington and disappeared behind a curtain.

"This is a madhouse!" Aunt Priscilla exclaimed. "Take me home."

"We have to get the ring off first," said Mrs. Osgood.

"*Next!*" Mrs. Sandsbury yelled.

"We're next!" Mrs. Osgood yelled back.

She grabbed Aunt Priscilla by the hand, dragged her to the admitting desk, and thrust her hand toward the clerk.

"We need to get this taken off," she announced.

"What did you have in mind?" asked Mrs. Sandsbury sarcastically. "Just a few fingers or the whole hand?"

Mr. Northington was wheeled back out then, his head and ankle bandaged, his face dotted with the heavy white cream that had been used to treat the stings.

"Could he talk again?" asks the girl.

"Not well," says the mother. "Yet he still had plenty to say."

As Priscilla was checking in at the desk, Northington overheard her name, and his ears perked up. He turned to the nurse who was walking him out.

Still struggling to speak with his swollen tongue, he asked, "Is that Prithilla Renthrough?"

"I shouldn't say," whispered the nurse. "But yes. She was quite famous back in the day. Nobody in town has seen her for years."

Then Mr. Northington spotted the Osgoods and the chief

of police he had met at the Osgoods' house. He rushed over to tell them what he knew.

"I know thomthing!" he shouted.

They all turned to look at him, and he was quite a sight: his hair was in disarray, his cheeks were swollen, his eyes were a watery red, and his bandaged tongue lolled partway out of his mouth as he spoke. At his feet, Muffin was nibbling on his bandaged ankle. But Mr. Northington was undeterred.

"I know where thee ith!" he shouted. "Anthabella!"

"He knows where she is!" shouted Mrs. Osgood.

And he pointed at Aunt Priscilla, who was being led out by another nurse.

"Thee's on her way to *her* howf. To Aunt Prithilla's."

"That's ridiculous," said the chief of police. "We've all just come from there, and Arabella was not with us."

"Just the other one," Mrs. Osgood sighed. "Just Henrietta."

"Henrietta!" Mr. Osgood said, realizing for the first time that they had forgotten all about her.

"Henrietta!" says the girl. "You never told me. What happened to Henrietta?"

## ARABELLA HESITATES

Henrietta was in a panic. As soon as the fire started, she ran to her room and slammed the door. She went to the window and tried to open it, but it was stuck. She was desperate to get the window open somehow, but there was nothing in the room she could think to use. Finally she was so terrified that she decided to kick out the glass. Then she stood at the window screaming for help as loudly as she possibly could.

What Henrietta didn't know, what almost no one knew at the time, was that Arabella was very near. In fact, Arabella and Gus had arrived at Aunt Priscilla's earlier and left again.

"What?" says the girl. "Why would they do that?"

"They had good reason," the mother replies.

The first time they arrived, they could hear the chief of police pounding on Aunt Priscilla's door from almost a block away. They froze in their tracks and crept forward slowly, doing their best not to be seen, which in Gus's case (as you can imagine) was a real challenge. As they got closer, they could make out voices and even words: "Aunt Priscilla" and "police."

"Wait here," Arabella said to Gus.

"Don't be ridiculous. I can't let you go over there alone."

"They'll see you," Arabella said.

"Good point," says the girl. "It's hard to miss a giant in a fuzzy pink sweater."

"True."

And that's why Arabella crept forward all alone just in time to see her parents, her nanny, her principal, and the chief of police enter the house on Chillington Lane without her.

Arabella could not believe her eyes. She turned on her heel and flew back to Gus.

"My parents are there!" she yelled. "And the police!"

"Calm down," said Gus.

"But what are they doing there? Do you think they're having Henrietta arrested?"

"Arrested?" laughed Gus. "Of course not! What for?"

"Then why?"

"I warned you before," said Gus. "They're probably looking for you."

As soon as he said it, Arabella knew Gus was right.

"I can't believe it," she said, tears welling in her eyes. "I've come all this way."

"I know," said Gus.

"Gus, I'm in big trouble. The police!"

"Let's just see if we can find out what's going on," said Gus.

And so they walked the rest of the way to Aunt Priscilla's house, hoping that nobody would spot them.

"Didn't anyone see?" asks the girl.

"No."

"Wouldn't they?"

"Nobody did. Not a soul. They were all alone. All alone in a world of very unobservant grown-ups."

"I know the feeling," says the girl.

Gus and Arabella reached Priscilla's house and tiptoed toward the front window. They desperately wanted to peek inside so they could figure out what was going on, but the curtains were pulled tight. They stood and stared at them helplessly for a few long moments, and then suddenly the curtains sprang apart. And Gus leapt to one side and Arabella to the other, like actors waiting in the wings at opposite ends of a stage. Through the window, Arabella could see her mother crying and the chief of police pacing the room.

"What are they saying?" Arabella whispered to Gus.

"I can't hear a thing. Just that little dog barking."

"That's Muffin," Arabella whispered.

They watched as the adults inside the dimly lit living room waved their arms and changed positions. Then there was a loud noise, and an alarming thing happened.

"What?" asks the girl.

"Don't you remember?" asks the mother. "Henrietta fell down the stairs."

Imagine how hard it was for Arabella. She had made such a long journey to see her sister, and at last she had arrived, but

181

she could not go inside to help her. Fortunately, Rose went to check on Henrietta, and shortly Arabella could see that her sister was all right. Arabella watched through the window as Henrietta approached the old woman.

"That must be her," she whispered to Gus. "That must be Aunt Priscilla."

Arabella was surprised Priscilla didn't look as scary as she had expected; at any rate, Henrietta didn't seem to be afraid of her. In fact, Henrietta was hugging the old woman. And then Priscilla began to pull at her hand. And then they all huddled around her, and there was more muffled yelling, as well as furious barking from Muffin.

"What are they doing?" Arabella whispered.

Gus shrugged, but then a second later he grabbed her hand. "They're coming toward the door!" Gus yelled. "Run!"

"They just left her there?" asks the girl. "After all that?"

"No," says the mother. "But they didn't want to get caught. They needed a plan."

Arabella and Gus ran across the street and hid behind a bush.

"They hid?"

"Yes, dear."

"Behind a bush?"

"Yes, dear."

"A giant was able to hide behind a bush."

"It was a large bush."

"Even so."

"It was getting dark, you must remember."

"Even so!"

"Well, they were all quite focused on getting Aunt Priscilla to the hospital. They considered it . . ."

". . . an emergency," says the girl with a sigh.

Gus and Arabella hid and watched the Osgoods and Rose and the chief of police and Principal Rothbottom and Aunt Priscilla pile into the car and head off, not understanding a bit of what they were seeing. Then they debated for a long while about what to do.

"Go," Gus said. "You've gotten this far. Now's your chance."

"What if they come back?" Arabella said.

"I'll keep watch for you," Gus told her.

"I don't know," said Arabella, hesitating.

"Arabella," said Gus sternly. "You can't lose heart now. Think how happy Henrietta will be to see you."

Arabella knew that he was right, but it took some time and a short walk for Gus to convince her.

"Please go with me," Arabella said when they returned, "to make sure they are gone."

And so they went together. And halfway back they saw and heard something that ended all hesitation: smoke was billowing out of Priscilla's house, and they could hear Henrietta yelling for help.

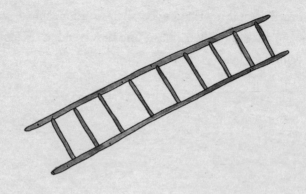

## ❧ A RESCUE AND A REUNION ☙

Arabella ran toward the house, calling out her sister's name and assuring her that she would save her. Arabella ran so fast, her lungs burned until she was, at last, standing beneath a huge arched window. Henrietta stood above her, framed in broken glass. They were both crying by now.

"It's going to be all right, Hen," Arabella assured her sister. "But you need to jump."

"I can't," said Henrietta. "I'm too scared."

They argued for a while, screaming back and forth: jump, I can't, jump, I can't, and so on. And it might have all ended very badly except for the fact that Gus was there to save the day.

"How?" asks the girl.

"How what?"

"How did he save the day, of course! Did he convince Henrietta to jump into his arms and escape?"

"No! He was tall, but not as tall as a house. He found a ladder and used that. Just as anyone else would."

"What about the house?"

"Well, honey, Gus was resourceful and brave, but he wasn't a firefighter, I'm afraid."

Henrietta, trembling, descended the ladder. At the bottom, Arabella was waiting. The girls threw their arms around each other, and Henrietta could feel her sister's tears dampening her neck.

"Don't cry," Henrietta told her. "It's all right now."

"Oh, Hen," Arabella said. "What have I done? This is all my fault."

"But you saved me, Bella!" Henrietta said. "I can't believe you're here."

"Of course I'm here. I had to find you."

"I hate to interrupt," Gus said, his deep voice startling them. "But I think we'd better go."

The house was fully in flames now, and the smoke was beginning to make them cough. Just then they heard the first fire truck come roaring toward them. A crowd began to form on the street.

"Stand back!" the firefighters yelled as they jumped off the truck.

"Aunt Priscilla's house!" Henrietta said sadly.

"The firefighters will do what they can," Gus said.

"Do you think they can save it?" Henrietta asked.

"I'm afraid it isn't likely," Gus answered.

"But where will we go?" asked Arabella.

Henrietta thought for a second and then suggested that they go to the bookshop.

"I know where Inez hides the spare key," Henrietta said. "And under the circumstances, I don't think she'll mind a bit if we let ourselves in."

. . .

Then they set off. Arabella, remembering her manners at last, introduced Gus to her sister. And Gus lifted the girls onto his shoulders and carried them all the way to the bookshop, where he gently set them down.

"I know this place!" Arabella exclaimed. "The woman who owns it helped me find you."

"I'm not surprised," said Henrietta. "She's been really kind to me."

Henrietta found the key and let them in, leading them through the soft darkness toward the back of the shop to Inez's office.

"Here," said Henrietta, handing the electric kettle to Gus. "Fill this, please, and I'll get us some cups for tea."

When Gus had walked away, Henrietta ran her fingers through her sister's too-short bangs.

"I'm sorry," she whispered.

"Me too, Hen," said Arabella.

Though they had spent their whole lives talking to each other, neither of them knew what else to say at that moment. So Henrietta lifted the dish of peppermints Inez kept on her desk and offered it to Arabella.

"Want one?" she asked.

"It's better than fish soup," Arabella said.

"How do you know about that?" Henrietta asked.

"I'm your sister, silly. I know everything about you."

When Gus returned, he found the girls smiling at one another, their faces so alike that he had to stop himself from staring.

They talked for a while longer until they grew sleepy and decided they should turn in for the night. The twins slept on the sofa, with their heads at opposite ends. Gus took off his sweater and threw it over them. They were warm and comfortable there and almost completely happy, because they were together again. Of course, it was hard not to worry about what would happen in the morning and whether they would be in trouble for running away or would be blamed for the fire, but it had been a very long day. And now they were able to forget it all for a while, just shut it out and close their eyes.

Gus had a harder time falling asleep. He was too big for the desk chair, and had to sit on the floor, and even then the only way he could stretch out his very long legs was to prop his head in the corner of the room and unfold his legs diagonally between the couch and the desk. Once he had arranged himself, he still couldn't rest because he was cold. Very cold. And then he got the idea to take down one of the drapes that hung on the window behind the desk. The drapes were made of green velvet, and they were warm and soft, the perfect blanket. And so, finally, they all fell asleep in the back office of the bookshop, their dreams as lovely as the stories in the books that surrounded them.

## ⟩⟩⟩ OFF WITH HER RING ⟨⟨⟨

While Gus and the girls were busy with the fire at Aunt Priscilla's, Aunt Priscilla herself was in an examining room at the hospital, waiting for the doctor who would remove the emerald ring from her swollen finger.

"Do we have to cut it off?" Mrs. Osgood kept asking the nurse who was taking Priscilla's temperature. "Nobody's going to want it if it's damaged."

"Oh, it has to come off," the nurse insisted. "And right away. People lose a digit this way all the time."

"A digit?" asks the girl.

"A finger," says the mother.

"Please tell me you're kidding," says the girl.

"I can hear you!" said Aunt Priscilla. "Stop nattering and go get the doctor!"

"The doctor will be here in a moment," said the nurse just as the doctor walked in.

"Well. Miss Larchmont," said the doctor with a smile. "Let's get you ready for surgery!"

"Surgery?" said Aunt Priscilla. "I'm not having surgery!"

"Now, now, Miss Larchmont, there's no need to be nervous. You'll feel much better once we remove that appendix, believe you me."

"The ring!" yelled Mrs. Osgood to the nurse. "Tell him about the ring."

"Miss Larchmont's ring—" the nurse began.

"My!" said the doctor. "I think that's the largest emerald I've ever seen."

"My name is not—" began Priscilla, who was suddenly interrupted by barking.

"Bad dog!" yelled Mrs. Osgood. "Muffin, come here!"

"You need to get that dog out of here," said the nurse. "We need to concentrate on Miss Larchmont now."

"*Stop!*" yelled Priscilla. "There is nothing wrong with my appendix, and my name is not Miss Larchmont!"

"I don't understand," said the doctor. "Where is Miss Larchmont?"

"Over here," said a voice from the next curtained cubicle.

"Excuse me," said the doctor, backing out of the exam area and entering the one next door.

"Well, Miss Larchmont!" they heard him say. "Let's get you ready for surgery!"

Aunt Priscilla rolled her eyes.

"Did they ever take the ring off?" asks the girl.

"They most certainly did. Another doctor came in at last and tended to Aunt Priscilla."

"That's good," says the girl.

"It was," says the mother. "Though the whole thing was a little hard on Miss Larchmont."

"Miss Larchmont?"

Over on her side of the curtains, Miss Larchmont was terribly nervous about her impending surgery, and unfortunately she had nothing better to do while she waited than to eavesdrop on what was happening to Aunt Priscilla.

"Let me see your finger," she heard the doctor say. "My, that is swollen. Don't worry. We'll have this cut off in no time."

"Please don't lose it!" Aunt Priscilla said.

"Of course not," said the doctor. "We'll put it in a bag so you can take it home with you."

"Nurse!" yelled Miss Larchmont. "I think I'm going to be sick."

Grinding sounds began in Aunt Priscilla's room.

"There you are," said the doctor. "Nothing to it, really."

"Nurse!" yelled Miss Larchmont. "I think I'm going to faint!"

## ≈: THE TRUTH COMES OUT :≈

In the waiting room, Mr. Osgood had begun to pace the floor, a worried crease forming in his brow.

"Relax," Mrs. Osgood told him. "Someone is bound to find Arabella any moment. The sketch I created looks just like her."

"If I may interrupt," said the chief of police, "I think we're going to need to redo those posters a bit."

"Why?" asked Mrs. Osgood. "I think they're perfect."

"We never listed the amount of the reward," said the chief. "And we need to mention the emerald ring. In fact, as long as we're making new posters, perhaps you have a photo of Arabella we might use?"

Mrs. Osgood glared at him, incensed at the implied criticism of her artistic ability.

"Or," said the chief, eager for any excuse to separate himself from Mrs. Osgood, "perhaps the school has something."

Meanwhile, Principal Rothbottom was proclaiming his innocence to an elderly couple.

"I mean, clearly the school is not at fault. But that's how it is these days! Parents expect the schools to practically raise their children for them. Never mind that they don't even bother keeping track of where said children are at any given hour of the day. . . ."

"Excuse me," said Mrs. Sandsbury. "Perhaps it would be better if you waited for their translator to arrive."

"Translator?" asked Principal Rothbottom.

"Yes. It might be best. Unless you speak Chinese."

"Oh," said Principal Rothbottom.

"You mean they didn't understand what he was saying?" says the girl.

"Not a word," says the mother.

"If you'll excuse me," said Rose to Mrs. Osgood, "I'd like to freshen up a bit." And she hurried away to the restroom to straighten her skirt and smooth her hair, because she hated to look a mess, and besides, the doctor was a very attractive fellow.

Unmoved by all the fuss, Mr. Osgood was quietly staring out the window, wondering where Arabella was and wishing that Aunt Priscilla would emerge soon so that they could take her home and check on Henrietta.

"Poor Henrietta," he thought guiltily. "We've forgotten you again."

"He misses her!" says the girl.

"I believe he was beginning to," says the mother.

He even went up to his wife and said, "I'm heading back to Priscilla's. We shouldn't have left Henrietta there all alone."

"She'll be fine," said Mrs. Osgood. "She's a very sensible little girl."

"Sensible?" asked Principal Rothbottom, butting into the conversation. "Mr. Stilton-Sterne informed me that the girl had attacked her sister with a pair of scissors."

"Well . . . ," said Mrs. Osgood.

"That's what you said in your note to the school," said Principal Rothbottom. "That Henrietta had attacked her sister. Disfigured her, I believe."

Aunt Priscilla emerged at that moment—newly ringless—

from the curtained room. "Osgood, you sent a violent criminal to live with me?"

"Of course not!" yelled Mr. Osgood.

"A violent criminal?" asked Rose, who had just returned. "Who's a violent criminal?"

"The Osgood girl," said the chief of police. "Why were we not informed of this alleged assault?"

"It wasn't that way!" said Mr. Osgood. "My wife was upset when she wrote that note."

"No good covering up for the girl," said the chief of police. "Best to come clean now."

"Are they talking about her bangs?" Rose asked Mrs. Osgood.

"I believe they are," said Mrs. Osgood.

She looked strange. If Rose hadn't known her better, she would have sworn that Mrs. Osgood was blushing with embarrassment.

"Now, now," said Rose, as if she were scolding children. "Stop this at once! Henrietta's no monster. I've helped raise her myself. I ought to know. She feels awful about cutting her sister's bangs."

"Cutting her bangs?" they all asked in unison.

"Why, yes. Isn't that what you're all talking about? She cut Arabella's bangs, and that's why—"

"Are you telling me," asked Aunt Priscilla, nearly trembling with rage, "that this *whole thing* was started by a *bad haircut*?!"

"Well," said Mrs. Osgood quietly, "it's possible that I may have overreacted."

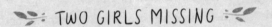 TWO GIRLS MISSING

"Aunt Priscilla," said Mr. Osgood in his most soothing voice, "let us take you home."

Aunt Priscilla, relieved as she was to have the ring off and her hand returning to normal, was in no mood to be taking orders from her nephew.

"Osgood," she said, "I have no intention of getting back into that car with the pack of you and that yippy little dog."

"Well, we can't leave you here," said Mr. Osgood. "After all you've been through."

"Osgood," said Aunt Priscilla. "I've been taking care of myself for years. I see no particular reason why I should stop right now."

Aunt Priscilla insisted that she would take a taxi home because she needed her beauty sleep and the whole thing had, after all, already been a horrible strain and inconvenience. And, in the end, they didn't even apologize for disturbing her and crashing into her house and coercing her out of her most prized possession, which Mrs. Osgood snatched just as they dashed out the door. Worse yet, in their haste they forgot Muffin, and Aunt Priscilla, sighing, had to grab the little dog and keep it with her.

. . .

"What happens next?" Mrs. Osgood asked as they drove away from the hospital.

"I thought we agreed to stop back at Priscilla's and check in on Henrietta before we head home," said Mr. Osgood.

"I'm sure she's fine," said Mrs. Osgood.

"It's on the way," said Mr. Osgood.

"That's what you always say!" said Mrs. Osgood, her exasperation evident to everyone in the car.

"Oh dear," whispered the nanny to the principal in the backseat.

"Precisely why I never married," the principal whispered in reply.

"I think we should check on the girl," said Principal Rothbottom in his most authoritative voice.

"Did he think something was wrong?" asks the girl.

"Not really. But who wants to listen to married people argue? Particularly when you're trapped in a car with them."

Now, the Osgoods enjoyed bickering as much as any long-married couple, but it had been a tiring day, and even Mrs. Osgood was beginning to feel a bit ashamed of leaving Henrietta behind. So at last they drove to Aunt Priscilla's house to check on Henrietta. Well, perhaps it would be more accurate to say that they drove to the spot where Aunt Priscilla's house used to stand. By the time they got there, the fire department was dousing the last of the flames.

"Henrietta!" screamed Mrs. Osgood, jumping from the car. "My baby!"

"Now she's concerned?"

"Well, she is the girl's mother."

"And she probably did feel a little guilty," says the girl.

"Mothers always do," says the mother.

"Are you the owners?" asked a firefighter.

"No," answered Mr. Osgood. "My aunt."

"Well, sir," the firefighter said. "I'm afraid the news is not good. The neighbors heard someone calling for help, but all we've been able to find is this."

And the firefighter held up one scorched shoe—a shoe far too small to belong to a grown woman.

Mrs. Osgood took one look at it and a single word escaped her lips: "Henrietta." Then she fainted into Mr. Osgood's arms.

## ❧ HOME ALONE ❧

The Osgoods were distraught, dazed by their misfortune. Two girls missing. And this last one—they had to admit—seemed entirely their fault. They had, after all, left the girl completely unattended.

"That man at the hospital . . . ," Mrs. Osgood said.

"Northington?" asked Principal Rothbottom.

"He was trying to tell us where Arabella is."

"I'm sure he has no idea," said Principal Rothbottom.

"Besides, my dear," said Mr. Osgood sadly, "he seemed to think that Arabella was here."

"Then it's really true. She's . . ." Mrs. Osgood, unable to finish, began to wail anew.

"You must get hold of yourself, ma'am," said the firefighter. "We aren't certain of anything yet. Our investigation is just beginning. Why don't you go home and get some rest?"

And as soon as he said it, they knew he was right. They had done all they could for one day, and so they headed home.

"That's sad," says the girl.

"It was," agrees the mother.

"And they didn't even wait for Aunt Priscilla to get home," says the girl.

"As usual," says the mother, "they were a bit too focused on themselves."

In all their panic over the twins, they had forgotten poor Priscilla, or at least left her to fend for herself. They piled back into the car, where they were all finally quiet on the ride to the Osgoods'. When they got home, the house looked lovely in the moonlight. It was a beautiful home, but empty now of the children who belonged there.

"We will find them," Mr. Osgood whispered to his wife as they waved goodbye to the principal and the chief of police and let themselves in through the front door.

"I guess you won't be needing me tomorrow," the nanny said.

"Nonsense," said Mr. Osgood. "Go and get a good night's sleep. We'll expect you bright and early."

## WIDE AWAKE

The Osgoods had a troubled, fitful sleep that night, exhaustion competing with worry. If only they could have known how cozy and safe their girls were—asleep in the bookshop—they would have smiled and rested. Instead, they tossed and turned and kept waking, expecting the morning, only to find that the most horrible night of their lives still had not ended.

And Mr. Northington—similarly ignorant of the girls' whereabouts—was also wide awake. When the Osgoods scoffed at his announcement that Arabella was heading to her aunt's house, Northington nearly gave up hope. He left the hospital and collected his dented tandem bicycle and began to pedal toward home, dejected.

"It's going to take me forever to get home, tired as I am," he thought. "Even if I don't dawdle."

And as soon as he had that thought, another struck him like a thunderbolt.

"That's it!" he shouted out loud to no one. "U-weeka!"

"What's wrong with him?" asks the girl.

"Nothing at all," says the mother. "Quite the contrary. He's had an epiphany."

"Like a seizure?"

"No, like a sudden realization."

Mr. Northington—despite his many limitations—had devoted many years to working with children. And much of that time had been spent trying to hurry them along in one way or another. He had prodded slow eaters to finish their lunches, rounded up stragglers who stuck to the edges of the playground after the bell had rung, and hustled the last few remaining children out of the school building at the end of each day, marveling at the trail of dropped homework papers they left in their wake. Northington knew how slow children could be, moving through the world on those smallish legs, constantly distracted by every rock and stick. And that is why Northington also knew—with complete certainty—that Arabella might still be on her way to Aunt Priscilla's house.

"Was she?" asks the girl.

"No," says the mother. "By the time Mr. Northington was having his . . ."

". . . epiphany . . ."

"Yes. Very nice. By then Gus and Arabella had already come and gone from Aunt Priscilla's."

And by the time Mr. Northington located Chillington Lane—a process that was greatly slowed by his garbled pronunciation—Gus and Arabella were huddled at the end of Priscilla's street, trying to determine if it was safe to go back and visit Henrietta. Northington was so excited when he spotted Arabella that he nearly fell off his bike. Arabella, on the other hand, was preoccupied with her conversation with Gus and didn't even notice him. So Northington was able to prop his bike against a tree and hide.

"He hid behind the tree?"

"He was a tall, lanky fellow," says the mother. "Picky eater as a child."

It was hard to see Arabella, clearly hidden as she was by that huge girl (or was it a woman?) in the floppy straw hat. But Northington studied the scene from his hiding spot. He wanted to grab Arabella immediately and order her onto the back of the rickety tandem bicycle to take her home, where he would be rewarded and welcomed as a hero. But that huge friend of hers looked like trouble. And so Northington hesitated.

"He was afraid of a girl?" asks the girl.

"Well, it wasn't *really* a girl, was it? It was Gus."

"In a stolen hat."

"Anyway," asks the mother, "aren't you the one who's always saying girls are just as tough as boys?"

"Continue," says the girl.

"You've come this far," Northington heard Arabella's huge friend say.

And soon Gus and Arabella were heading past him down the road. Northington followed on foot, running in short spurts behind them, concealing himself at every opportunity behind bushes and trees and lampposts.

"Lampposts?" asks the girl.

"Rather ineffective, I must admit."

But Gus and Arabella were too distracted by the fire and Henrietta's cries for help to notice anything else. Northington watched from across the road as the Osgood girls yelled to one another. He saw Gus prop the ladder against the house. He saw the fire trucks arrive. Throughout it all, he knew that he ought to move. He was the adult, and they—possibly even that huge creature in the hat—were children.

"Why didn't he help them?" asks the girl.

"He was afraid," says the mother. "And unsure of what to do."

"But he's the principal!" says the girl.

"Assistant principal," reminds the mother. "And the truth is that the people in charge are often afraid and uncertain."

"So he did nothing?"

"No. As they left, he followed them. After all, he made his living being suspicious about what children might be up to."

Northington followed them to the bookshop. He watched them enter, then wrote down the address in a small notebook he always kept in his back pocket to record the names of children who needed to be sent to Principal Rothbottom's office. Then, as Gus and Arabella and Henrietta settled in to sleep, Northington pedaled home under the full moon, secure in the knowledge that by morning he could reveal all to the Osgoods and the police. He would be a hero. Miss Dewey would be unspeakably impressed by his gallant rescue of the missing girl. Exhausted as he was, he forged ahead, imagining a ceremony at which the mayor pinned a medal to his chest as Miss Dewey sat clapping in the front row.

## PRISCILLA RENFREW
## MEETS HER MATCH

Like all the others, Aunt Priscilla had had a very long night. She had been accosted by relatives, had surrendered her precious emerald ring, and had been abandoned at the hospital with Muffin, who was clearly the world's most troublesome little lapdog. And the worst was yet to come. As there was only one cab driver in town, and a rather unreliable one at that, Priscilla waited for hours, dozing in the hospital lobby. Finally she decided to walk back home, carrying the whimpering Muffin in her arms.

"Couldn't she just say a spell and transport herself there?" asks the girl.

"Or fly there on a broom, right?" asks the mother.

"Yes."

"How many times must I tell you that she's not a witch? She had to walk. And it was very slow going too because she's an older woman."

"Poor Priscilla," says the girl.

Aunt Priscilla walked a very long time; the sun began to come up. And at some point she saw a fire engine stopped at a red light. She decided to ask them if . . .

"Stopped at a red light?" asks the girl.

"Well, they were on the way back from the fire, dear. No need to run red lights at that point, is there?"

Priscilla asked them if they might give her a ride home, and they said they were sorry but they were going the other way.

"We're on our way back from a house fire," they said. "Big gray Victorian at the end of Chillington Lane."

"Gray?" asked Priscilla, her voice starting to shake.

"Yes. Shame it burned down; we tried our best. Worst part is we couldn't find the old woman who lives there. Everybody says she hasn't left the house in years, and of course that leaves us to imagine. . . . Well, nobody's exactly crying big crocodile tears about losing her, though, if you know what I mean."

Priscilla had turned pale.

"Ma'am?" asked the firefighter. "Are you okay?"

Of course Priscilla recognized the description of herself and her house. She thought for a moment about bursting into tears, but that wasn't her way. So, instead, she turned toward the firefighters and pointed a long, crooked finger at them. Then she began to shout.

"You fools! You incompetent fools! Are you trying to tell me that the first time in . . . in a *very* long time that I have left my house, the pack of you have managed to let it burn to the ground?"

"Sorry, ma'am," the firefighter yelled down to her from the engine's cab.

"We have to get going. Need to check in at the station," added his partner, who was driving.

Then they switched on the siren and sped away.

"But it wasn't an emergency anymore," says the girl.

"I think they really wanted to get away from her," says the mother.

"Poor Priscilla."

She was a pathetic sight. "Stop!" she was yelling. Also "You will pay for this!" and other threatening things. They really didn't hear much of it, given their loud and hasty exit. Eventually, Priscilla's noisy and hostile complaints trailed off to a pathetic whimper. She sat down at the edge of the dusty roadway on the curb, where she did, finally, and perhaps for the first time in her life, begin to cry.

"Why me?" she wailed. "Why me? I'm a good person!"

"She really is," says the girl to her mother. "She did give up the ring to save Arabella."

"She did indeed," says the mother.

Priscilla cried and muttered loudly about how this is what happened to you when you spent your time trying to help distant relatives, and wasn't it enough that she had taken in Osgood's daughter, who (though she really wasn't as bad as she had seemed at first) was no help around the house and couldn't even cook a simple meal. And now, because of the other one, she was away at the wrong moment and had lost everything. *Everything*. It was simply too much. Even their ridiculous, noisy little dog had abandoned her. It was, at that moment, fading off into the distance, still running, barking, following the fire engine.

Then Priscilla had an even darker thought.

"Henrietta!" she cried. "Henrietta was in the house! Oh no!"

And she covered her face and sobbed.

She was weeping and muttering Henrietta's name when she felt a tap on her shoulder and heard a small, timid voice ask her, "Aunt Priscilla? Aunt Priscilla, are you all right?"

Aunt Priscilla jumped up at the sound of Henrietta's voice. Her eyes grew wide as if she were seeing a ghost. She reached out and pinched Henrietta's arm.

"Ouch!" Henrietta yelled.

"Oh, good!" cried Priscilla. "You're real."

"Of course I'm real," said Henrietta. "We came to check on you."

Arabella and Henrietta and Gus had gotten up early that morning, and finding that they were too hungry to make a breakfast of tea and peppermint candy, and feeling guilty that they had not stayed long enough to see what had happened to Priscilla and her burning house, they had decided to walk back to find out.

"You must be the sister," Priscilla said, pointing at Arabella. "You, young lady, have been the cause of quite a lot of trouble. Aren't you supposed to be missing?"

"All I wanted was to find my sister," Arabella said. Arabella explained the long journey she had made to find her twin.

"So you're a runaway!" Pricilla shouted. "A runaway!

I might have known. And I've gone to all this trouble to try to help you when you didn't need help. When what you *needed* was to be severely punished. And you shall be; I can promise you that!"

"Miss Renfrew," said Gus. "If I may be so bold as to interrupt . . ."

"He's very polite, isn't he?" asks the girl.

"He's a gentle giant," replies her mother.

Gus went on to explain, in the mildest possible terms, that Priscilla had other problems; for example, her house had burned, right to the ground.

"I know that!" yelled Priscilla. "Do you think I need you to come along and explain it all to me? If I hadn't been out of the house, running to the hospital after nearly destroying my hand to give up valuable property to help find nieces who aren't really missing, who deserve to be *throttled* . . ." And then she stopped. "I'm so confused," she said. And she burst into tears again.

Henrietta felt sorry for Priscilla, in spite of all the horrible food and the drafty, creepy bedroom. Gus felt even worse, and he gathered her up and carried her the rest of the way in his arms as you would carry a tired and cranky child off to bed. He didn't put her down until they reached her house. Or, to be more exact, the place where her house had been. What was left was a still-smoking pile of rubble and a few crumbling, blackened walls. Black cats were wandering through the sooty debris, mewing.

"Oh dear," said Priscilla when she saw it. "Oh dear, look at this. Look at this!"

And the four of them did just that: stood there with mouths hanging open, wondering what to do next.

## ❧ THE RETURNING HERO ❧

Mr. Northington, who had arrived home in the wee hours of the morning, was up early after a short nap. He knotted his tie, carefully combed his sparse hair, and presented himself at the Osgoods' front door at an inappropriately early hour. Mr. Osgood, the only member of the household who was awake, seemed confused to see him there.

"Yes?" he said, opening the door just a crack.

Mr. Northington smiled widely and patted himself on the chest. "Excellent news, Mr. Osgood!" he said, entirely too loudly. "Excellent news! I know where they are."

Mr. Osgood was trying to recall who this lunatic on his

front steps was. "Oh, yes," he said. "Mr. Northington. From the school."

"At your service," said Mr. Northington.

"Listen, Mr. Northington," said Osgood, "I don't mean to be rude, but my wife and I have been through quite an ordeal and—"

"Visitors?" asked Rose sleepily as she joined Mr. Osgood in the doorway. "Would you like some tea?"

"Yes!" said Northington.

"No!" said Mr. Osgood.

"What's all the shouting?" asked Mrs. Osgood, descending the stairs in her blue robe, wiping sleep from her eyes.

"She's never getting dressed, is she?"

"That was really the least of her worries," says the mother.

"Mr. Northington, I think it would be best—" Mr. Osgood tried again.

"The man from the hospital!" Mrs. Osgood shouted. "Let him in!"

"Tea?" asked Rose.

"Yes!" said Northington, smiling.

"No!!" said Mr. Osgood.

But Rose was already leading Northington into the

living room. "We're so grateful," she was saying, "for any help we can get."

"Whatever I can do to assist," said Northington, gazing into Rose's (very blue) eyes.

"Do you know anything?" Mrs. Osgood asked. "About either of my girls?"

Northington cleared his throat and settled back into a lovely wingback chair; he was just about to answer when the doorbell rang again.

"Excuse me," said Mr. Osgood.

By now there was quite a ruckus outside. Through the Osgoods' front window, Northington spotted a clump of newcomers on the front porch. Principal Rothbottom and the chief of police stood nearly shoulder to shoulder with a smallish child squirming between them. As Mr. Osgood opened the front door, the chief of police was yelling, "We'll take this from here, Rothbottom."

"Unhand her," Principal Rothbottom was saying.

"Arabella!" Mrs. Osgood exclaimed, dashing toward the door.

In another moment, all of them had tumbled into the Osgoods' living room.

"That's right!" said the chief of police proudly. "We've found her! We've found your girl!"

"What?" asked Mr. Northington. "No! *I've* found her! I have the address right here!"

Mrs. Osgood, who by now had pushed her way through the crowd and grabbed the small personage in question, screamed, "You *absolute idiots*! That's not Arabella! That's not Henrietta either!"

"Are you sure?" asked the chief of police. "She looks just like the sketch."

"Oh, for pity's sake," said Rose. "Hand me that child. What's your name, love?"

"Waaaaah," sobbed Eliza.

"Wanda?" guessed the chief of police.

The nanny rolled her eyes. "Give us a moment, would you?" she asked.

"Eh, eh, eh," heaved Eliza, who was beginning to hyperventilate.

"Elmira!" yelled Mr. Northington. "I'm certain her name is Elmira."

"Elvira," corrected Principal Rothbottom.

"There, there, calm down, dear. Just breathe," said Rose. "Why don't you come and sit down, and we'll get you some tea and a biscuit."

"A biscuit!" snorted Mrs. Osgood. "Look, you, if you know anything about this, you better start talking."

Eliza sniffed and said, "My name is Eliza Sneedle, and I've only come to say that I'm sorry. We never should have done it."

"Done what?" Mrs. Osgood asked.

And Eliza started to weep again so loudly that it was left to Principal Rothbottom to explain how the children had concealed Arabella's absence by answering for her during roll call that fateful day.

"I knew that!" yelled Northington. "I'm the one who told you that! I have interviewed this child extensively and—"

"Northington," said Principal Rothbottom, "kindly let me handle this."

"So this really isn't your daughter?" asked the chief of police.

"*No!*" said the Osgoods in unison.

Then the room grew quiet for a second, and Northington seized his opportunity. Drawing himself up to his full height and raising one finger up in the air, he loudly proclaimed once more, "I know where the Osgood girls are!"

But his words were drowned out by the sound of a siren as a fire truck screeched to a stop in front of the house. And when the front door opened a third time, Henrietta, Arabella, and Gus stepped through.

"But how?" asks the girl.

"The firefighters had returned to check the scene, and they offered them a ride home."

"Poor Northington," says the girl.

"Poor Northington," the mother agrees.

But even Northington was moved by the girls' reunion with their parents. Mrs. Osgood rushed to the door and threw her

arms around both daughters. For once, she was at a loss for words.

"I'm glad to be home," said Henrietta.

"Can she stay?" asked Arabella.

"Of course," said Mrs. Osgood softly. "This is where she belongs."

And Mr. Osgood smiled and patted their heads.

"I can't find my handkerchief," said the chief of police.

"You can't find anything," said Mrs. Osgood, but she was smiling now, and the edge was gone from her voice.

The room grew so quiet then that they were all startled to hear a soft knock on the door.

"Who can that be?" asked Mr. Osgood. "The whole town is already here."

"Inez!" said Henrietta, pushing toward the door as soon as she spotted her friend. "I'm so glad you came!"

"Well," said Inez, "once I heard about the fire, I had to make sure you were okay. I wanted you to know Aunt Priscilla has decided to stay with me for a while."

"How good of you to come and tell us," said Mr. Osgood.

"How could I stay away?" She smiled. "You know how I love a good story."

## 🌿 A FRESH START 🌿

Sometimes a disaster is just a disaster, and nothing good can be said about it. But sometimes a disaster is an excuse for a fresh start. And that was the case for the Osgoods and Aunt Priscilla and all the others.

The next morning, while Mr. Osgood prepared to leave for the office, Mrs. Osgood sat down at her desk to write a note to Principal Rothbottom. This is what it said:

. . .

*Dear Principal Rothbottom,*

*Please excuse my daughters' recent absence from school. We appreciate anything you can do to help the girls catch up on their studies.*

*Sincerely,*

*Mrs. Osgood*

"They must be so far behind!" says the girl.

"They were. But fortunately Miss Dewey offered to tutor them in the library and help them compensate for the missing work. In fact, the girls, with some help from Miss Dewey, created a scrapbook of their travels to make up for the assignments they missed in school."

"Did they get extra credit?"

"Of course not! They had skipped homework and behaved badly here and there. But really it was a lovely book, with a pale blue cover and ivory pages. All hand-stitched. The girls asked Inez to help illustrate. Here, let me show you."

"It's beautiful," says the girl. "They must have been so proud."

"Children are capable of amazing things," says the mother.

"How good to hear you admit that," says the girl. "But, Mother . . ."

"Yes?"

"Where did you get it?"

"From your grandmother, of course. When they were done making it together and had read it many nights at home, Arabella and Henrietta gave it back to Miss Dewey."

"You mean Miss Dewey was . . ."

"Your grandmother, dear. Dewey was her maiden name—before she married. She added the book to the library. In fact, it was her favorite story there. And when she retired, she took it with her and gave it to me. It's yours now, if you want it."

"Really?" asks the girl, taking the pale blue book in her hands.

"Of course," says the mother.

"How did the story end?" asks the girl. "For the others?"

Well, Aunt Priscilla didn't weep forever about the fire. It was a huge loss, of course. All her familiar surroundings were gone. And the cats, disloyal creatures in the end, wandered away and never returned. And, of course, there was the expense.

"Didn't she have insurance or something?"

"That would have been handy, but no," says the mother.

"But she still had her fortune, right?"

"Well, it had dwindled over the years. But she did have her emerald ring. Until she had to sell it."

"How awful!" says the girl.

"Not really," the mother says.

In fact, the fire was in some ways the best thing that could have happened to Priscilla. After all, there's no better cure for fearing the world than having your house burn down. It rather forces you outside and back into life. And that is what happened with Aunt Priscilla Renfrew. Once she had ventured outdoors, she underwent an almost magical transformation; everything about her life began to change. She found a new place to live, of course—a small cottage near the center of town. And for the first time, she came to know her neighbors. She even discovered that some of them, like Inez and the goat tender Arabella had met, knew of her former glory on the stage. With their encouragement and support, and the money she got from the ring, Priscilla eventually opened up the Emerald Theater, where she staged plays and gave acting lessons. The Osgood sisters visited in the summers and helped with larger productions in exchange for voice and acting lessons from their aunt, who never asked either of them to cook.

"What about Gus?" asks the girl.

"I was just getting to him," replies her mother. "Gus returned home to find that his parents had decided to get a divorce."

"That's not a very happy ending," protests the girl.

"Well, sometimes that's the happiest ending that's possible."

Gus lived with his mother for a few years until he was old enough to venture out on his own. Then he left the nest and joined the circus. In fact, he rose through the ranks, or the rings, or whatever, until he was the ringmaster. It was quite good publicity for the circus, having a giant for a ringmaster,

and finally Gus felt that he had a place in the world that was large enough, so to speak.

"And the Osgoods?"

"Well, the first problem they had was to find a new nanny. Rose left to marry Mr. Northington within a month of the girls' return."

"Mr. Northington! But he was in love with Miss Dewey!"

"He was. But he and Rose began to talk after school each day when she came to collect the Osgood girls. And soon Rose proved a more appreciative audience for Mr. Northington than Miss Dewey had ever been."

"That's so fickle!" protests the girl.

"You should be happy for him," scolds the mother. "He finally had someone to ride with him on that tandem bicycle!"

"And Henrietta and Arabella?"

"Well, they went back to being sisters. And not just sisters, but best friends."

"Your sister can't be your best friend," says the girl.

"I beg to differ," says the mother. "Your sister can always be your best friend. After all, you have each other for your whole lives."

After their misadventure, Henrietta and Arabella got along a good deal better than they ever had before. By running away, Arabella had proven two things: that she loved her sister deeply and that she was not always perfect. And Henrietta had been missed during her time away and was therefore truly treasured when she returned.

## HOME AT LAST

And so it ends, in front of the fire, the story of two twin sisters and the adventures they shared with their parents, their aunt Priscilla, and their good friend Gus. The girls lived happily together in a lovely country house with a beautiful garden, where yellow roses perfumed the air. You can see them there, through the huge arched window, their heads bent close together in the lamplight, reading. It is a story of their own creation, full of the magic and misadventure of their lives.

# ❦ ACKNOWLEDGMENTS ❦

Many thanks to two early readers, Karen DeBrulye Cruze and Gay Lynn Cronin, talented writers and librarians, for getting me started. I am beyond grateful to my amazing agent, Miriam Altshuler, for her wise, skilled, and patient guidance at every stage of this book.

I am indebted as well to Michelle Frey, my kind and gifted editor at Knopf, and to everyone on the Knopf team, including Katrina Damkoehler, Artie Bennett, and Patricia Callahan.

And many thanks to Júlia Sardà for her beautiful illustrations.

I am grateful to my family for their enthusiasm and support. Michael, Liz, Bob, Judy, Eileen, Nick, Mary, and Kerry, you are the best siblings and in-laws on the planet.

Finally, and most importantly, I want to thank my husband, Gerry, and our sons, Sean and Jack, whose love and confidence in me make all things possible.

## ABOUT THE AUTHOR

Kathryn Siebel teaches humanities at Billings Middle School in Seattle and works with elementary school students at the Green Lake School-Age Care Program. She has worked in educational publishing and as an English teacher and librarian and has an MFA from the Iowa Writers' Workshop.

Kathryn lives with her family in Seattle. *The Trouble with Twins* is her first novel. You can find out more about Kathryn at kathrynsiebel.com.

## ABOUT THE ILLUSTRATOR

Júlia Sardà is an illustrator with a background in fine and graphic arts. She has also worked as a colorist in a studio affiliated with Disney/Pixar. Today she mostly does illustration for children's books, including some of her own childhood favorites: *Alice's Adventures in Wonderland*, *The Wonderful Wizard of Oz*, and *Charlie and the Chocolate Factory*.

Júlia lives in Barcelona, Spain. You can find out more about her work at juliasarda.com.

# YEARLING

*Turning children into readers for more than fifty years.*

**Classic and award-winning literature for every shelf.
How many have you checked out?**

**Find the perfect book, play games,
and meet favorite authors at RHCBooks.com!**